Max let a few seconds tick by before asking once again, "Truth or dare."

"Dare," she answered immediately, welcoming the change of subject from Max's "plans" for her. Now wishing she hadn't asked about that in the first place.

"You should have picked truth," he said. "Sure you don't want to change your mind?"

He still hadn't touched her, but the sexual tension was back. Buzzing between them like an electric magnet.

Pru's legs began to feel a little weak, but she shook her head in answer to his question. The old Pru wouldn't have backed down.

There came a moment of silence so suspended, it made Pru feel as if she were at the top of a roller coaster. Then he said, "Dance with me."

He reached into the basket and pulled out his phone. A few seconds later, it played a fairly new club anthem that Pru recognized from the night of their nightclub wedding.

Dear Reader,

As my longtime readers know, I don't write heroes—
I turn villains into heroes, in the hottest ways possible.
Max Benton, the playboy brother of Cole Benton
from *Vegas Baby*, happens to be one of my favorite
turns, because he's a bad boy to the core. Disreputable,
dishonorable, distressingly hot—and totally unapologetic
about it.

I hope you enjoy watching Max get exactly what he
deserves in Pru, a righteous and bodacious heroine, who's
about to turn his self-serving world inside out.

Love,

Theodora

Love's GAMBLE

THEODORA TAYLOR

HARLEQUIN® KIMANI™ ROMANCE

Recycling programs
for this product may
not exist in your area.

ISBN-13: 978-0-373-86412-6

Love's Gamble

Copyright © 2015 by Theodora Taylor

For questions and comments about the quality of this book please contact us
at CustomerService@Harlequin.com.

H HARLEQUIN®
™ www.Harlequin.com

Printed in U.S.A.

Love's GAMBLE

THEODORA TAYLOR

HARLEQUIN® KIMANI™ ROMANCE

Recycling programs
for this product may
not exist in your area.

ISBN-13: 978-0-373-86412-6

Love's Gamble

Copyright © 2015 by Theodora Taylor

HARLEQUIN®

www.Harlequin.com

Printed in U.S.A.

Theodora Taylor writes hot books with heart.
When not reading, reviewing or writing, she enjoys
spending time with her amazing family, going on date
nights with her wonderful husband, and attending parties
thrown by others. Visit her at theodorataylor.com and at
facebook.com/theodorataylorauthor.

Books by Theodora Taylor

Harlequin Kimani Romance

Vegas, Baby
Love's Gamble

Visit the Author Profile page at
Harlequin.com for more titles.

To everyone who asked me about Max and Pru.
Here you go!

Chapter 1

Tracking down Max Benton would involve walking straight into a den of temptation. Of course it would.

Pru could practically feel the bass from the nightclub's music entering her body through her feet and rocking its way up to her hips. The music came courtesy of Mike Benz, an up-and-coming half Dutch, half Cameroonian DJ who was enjoying his first stateside residency at Sin, one of New Orleans's premier nightclubs. His beats were fantastically good. So good, they awakened a long-dormant urge within Pru to get out on the crowded dance floor.

Back in the day it hadn't taken more than a glass of champagne and the right song to get Pru on the floor. And she'd often stayed there all night, enjoying bottle service courtesy of her latest boyfriend or admirer, dancing with her fellow showgirls until she couldn't dance anymore. Back in the day, her number-one goal in life had been to squeeze as much fun as she possibly could into her twenties, and to prove to everyone she came in contact with that Prudence Washington was the exact opposite of her boring name.

She was no longer a showgirl or hell-bent on proving that there was nothing prudent about her. Nonetheless, she was currently dressed to party well, in a little gold minidress pulled the day before from her mother's vintage collection of seventies-era cocktail attire. She considered it a uniform, the uniform she needed to get her job done. Her current job being Max Benton. And she was all about her job, which was why instead of hopping on the dance floor, she headed straight for VIP.

The hulking security guard standing at the bottom of the roped-off stairs that led up to the VIP area gave her an approving once-over as she approached. She must have had a little of the old Pru magic leftover, she thought.

She'd made the right choice. In the background, she heard the DJ announce that he was taking a break but would be back on the turntables before the night was through. Then his excellent beats were replaced by canned Top 40 music playing at even higher decibels.

"You on the list, baby?" the security guard asked, lifting up his clipboard.

She threw him a flirty look. "Not quite," she admitted. "The guy I'm here to see is trying to stay under the radar these days, but if you tell Max Benton that Prudence Washington is down here looking for him, I'm sure he'll appreciate you letting him know. *Really appreciate it.*"

The security guard didn't respond quite as hoped to her insinuation that there would be a nice tip involved if he passed along her message to Maxwell Benton, the younger, not nearly as responsible, Benton hotels heir. Not only did his face harden, he moved to stand between her and the black velvet rope.

"No Maxwell Benton here," he said, his voice completely monotone.

"Are you sure about that?" she asked. "Because I know he'll be upset if he hears I was asking for him and you didn't let me up."

She hoped.

The truth was, she was banking an awful lot on the fact that Max Benton had stepped to her twice. The first time had been at his brother Cole's wedding to her best friend, Sunny Johnson, about a year ago. The second time had been a couple of months ago, right before Pru's retirement from the Benton Revue, at Cole and Sunny's baby shower.

Shortly after the shower, Cole had cut his younger brother off, refusing to keep issuing checks for the brand-ambassador job he'd been assigned. Back when the Benton had been one luxury hotel, having an international playboy as the brand ambassador had been a good idea. Max had been all too happy to gallivant around the world, living the kind of life that perfectly encapsulated the particular decadent brand of luxury the Benton was trying to sell to its affluent guests and gamblers.

But then their grandfather had died, and Cole had taken over the Benton Group. He'd expanded the Benton from one hotel into a nationwide outfit of luxury casino resorts, which served to draw even more attention to Max's international escapades. Which wouldn't have been a problem, except then Cole started making plans for the Benton Inns, a new chain of midrange hotels that would cater to non-gambling clientele whose pockets weren't deep enough to afford a stay at one of the Benton Group's luxury properties. This new market expansion meant that Max's infamous reputation was no longer compatible with the Benton brand.

According to Cole, Max had stormed out of Vegas soon after Cole gave him the news about being fired. He sold all his stock in the Benton Group to some investment-fund manager before Cole could buy him out and then disappeared from the public eye. The only contact he'd had from Max since his departure from Vegas was a CC: on a short email, sent to their family's lawyers, informing them that he would like his trust paid out in full on his thirty-fifth birthday.

After receiving Max's email, Cole had hired a number of private investigators to track him down. To his surprise, they'd failed, finding neither hide nor hair of the play-boy who'd apparently decided to step out of the spotlight as soon as he was fired. The weeks until Max's birthday were ticking down now, which was why Cole had decided to let Pru, who was currently studying to take the private-investigator exam in the fall, have a shot at it. A long shot on his part, but a possibly huge opportunity for Pru. One she was taking seriously, since it was just the kind of case she needed to kick off her post-showgirl career.

After a week of trying to track down Max Benton from the one-bedroom apartment she shared with her brother, she'd decided to use her own limited funds to follow a hunch. Max, who had often been photographed with DJ Mike Benz in European nightclubs, would surely put in an appearance at his friend's very first stateside gig.

However, showing up here had been only a hunch, and she knew that there was a good chance the security guard wasn't lying about Max not being up in the VIP area. But then again, why would the guy have gone so cold on her if Max Benton weren't up there?

No, she thought, she'd definitely come to the right place. She could feel it in her gut. But how was she going to convince the mountain standing in front of her to let her through?

The mountain, who was currently saying, "Time for you to move along, ma'am."

Wow. Now he was calling her "ma'am"? That was past cold.

"Look," she said, leveling with him, "I know you have your orders, but—"

"Hallo, who are you?" someone interrupted before she could finish.

Mike Benz appeared beside her in a ratty purple hoodie and a T-shirt with a panda on it. His clothes, paired with his tall, thin frame, made him look even younger than Jakey, her eighteen-year-old brother. But Pru knew from her research that despite his youthful appearance, he was the same age as her, twenty-nine.

So at least she didn't feel like a shameless cradle robber when she turned on her old showgirl smile at full beam and said, "Hi! I'm Pru. I *love* your music."

She limited herself to those three sentences and held her breath. She'd hoped that the simple act of introducing herself with a big smile and an emphatic compliment would have the same effect it did back when she actually made a game out of getting into VIP.

It did.

Mike Benz smiled back at her and said, "Would you like to come up?"

"Sure!" she said, her smile becoming even brighter.

He offered her his arm, and with a sheepish look, the mountain unlatched the velvet rope before stepping aside to let them pass.

Just like that she was in! Pru's heart beat in her throat as they came to the top of the stairs. Hoping hard that her gut had been right and that Max Benton really was there tonight.

"M.B.!" a voice boomed across the area.

Mike Benz threw his arms in the air and yelled back "M.B.!" like a kid playing a game of Marco Polo.

Pru had to work hard to keep a triumphant smile from breaking out across her face. She had bet right. Max Benton approached them, dressed in a white linen suit with a V-neck T-shirt underneath. His on-trend look, paired with intentionally scruffy black hair and at least three days' worth of beard growth, somehow managed to make him look as if he'd rolled out of bed and a high-fashion ad at the same time. It was easy for Pru to understand in that moment why women around the world had fallen at Max Benton's feet. Why, according to the nauseating amount of research she'd done on the Benton heir, he'd been dubbed the Ruiner in certain feminine circles.

One reality starlet had claimed she wasn't able to date anyone for a year after spending a few weeks with Max. Pru remembered her tale with an inner grimace. *Once you go Max, you never go back.*

"I didn't know you were here," Mike Benz said to Max

as they clasped hands and exchanged a one-armed hug. "Why didn't you text me?"

Max threw him a lazy smile, his pale green eyes shining with their usual wicked gleam. "Figured you'd get up here sooner or later," he answered.

Pru watched the exchange from her position on Mike Benz's arm. Max was so insanely good-looking, even more so in real life than in the many pictures of him floating around the internet. If not for the jagged imperfection of his nose, which had been broken a couple of times without proper resets, Max might have been too pretty. But as it was, the crooked nose on top of so much symmetry only made it that much harder for Pru not to stare at him, even though she was trying to play it cool.

Max, however, didn't seem to have any problems keeping his eyes off her. He barely spared her a look while he and Mike Benz exchanged small talk about how Mike liked New Orleans. Pru was actually beginning to think that Max didn't remember her and she'd have to awkwardly reintroduce herself, when he said to Mike, "So you know Pru, too?"

He still hadn't looked directly at her, Pru noticed.

"Ya, man, we met outside VIP," Mike Benz answered.

Pru quickly rushed in then with her cover story. "One of the girls I used to dance with back in Vegas moved out to Miami and decided to have her bachelorette weekend here in New Orleans." This much was true—even if that bachelorette night had happened years ago, not tonight as Pru had insinuated.

"Anyway, I was pretty sure you were up here in the VIP area even though the guy downstairs kept saying you weren't." She squinched her face to further sell the story. "Trina's bachelorette weekend was wild, so I almost believed him. Like maybe I'd just been crazy, thinking it was you up here and not some other guy that maybe looked like you."

She held her breath, hoping Max didn't see straight through her technically-true-but-not-really story.

Max pegged her with a look, his eyes shrewd, as if he was deciding whether or not to believe her. But then he said, "No, it was me you saw, and I'm glad you decided to bring the party up here."

"Me, too." She turned to give Mike Benz another one of her showgirl smiles. "Thanks, Mike!"

Mike grinned down at her. "No problem. Any friend of the other M.B. is most definitely a friend of mine."

"Oh, goody," she said, doing her best imitation of the coquette she used to be. "I *love* making new friends."

She could sense Max watching her closely as she and Mike made flirty exchanges. This was another huge gamble. Openly flirting with someone else in order to get his attention. But from what she'd read, Max had a competitive streak a mile wide. In his twenties he'd drag raced on every continent except Antarctica. In his thirties, he'd been spotted at high-roller games with million-dollar stakes. And just a few weeks before Cole had cut him off, a story had surfaced about Max wagering the Benton New Orleans in a bet with another hotel heir about who could swim one hundred meters faster. Luckily he'd won that bet, considering he didn't have the authority to make that kind of wager in the first place.

But in any case, Pru sensed the easiest way to engage Max was to play to his sense of competition. And apparently she was right.

Max looped an arm around Pru's shoulders and said, "I've got a couple of bottles back at my table. Let's catch up, Pru."

Then he nodded toward Mike Benz and said, "You can join us if you want."

An hour later, Pru wasn't so sure who was scheming on whom. The three of them were sitting on a plush white couch, arced around a small table with a silver bucket full of ice and champagne bottles at its center. Max had his hand on her knee as he once again filled her glass with champagne. He'd yet to let her glass get more than half-empty. But as attentive as he'd been, he'd spent most of the night talking with Mike Benz about a hotel he was planning to build in New Orleans.

He'd explained the boutique hotel would sit somewhere between its luxury and lower-tier counterparts. With an Old World Parisian aesthetic outside, and a modern European design inside, the planned hotel would also have a hot nightclub that would attract and cater to the many singletons and unmarried couples who flooded into New Orleans every weekend, looking to have fun. Apparently, Max wasn't as disconnected from the experience of the non-VIP nightclubber as she would have thought, because he painted a picture of a trendy and sophisticated hotel with prices within reach of people in their twenties who hadn't been born with silver spoons in their mouths.

Pru could actually imagine herself going out of her way to stay at a place like that back when she'd been in her early twenties. It was also a very intriguing idea, coming from Max, since his hotel would probably be competing with both the Benton New Orleans and the planned Benton Inn New Orleans, which would be opening its doors in the fall.

She didn't have to fake her interest in the conversation. In fact, she had to keep reminding herself to surreptitiously pour out half flutes of champagne whenever both men weren't looking (with a silent apology to whomever was in charge of cleaning the club's carpets at night's end). And by the time Max was done telling Mike Benz about his plans, both she and the DJ were leaning all the way forward.

Max eventually asked Mike about his plans after his residency was through, and Mike confessed he didn't have any. By the time Mike's break was over, the two had all but made a formal deal for Mike Benz to be the first resident DJ at the hotel Max would be opening.

Pru observed Max as he watched Mike Benz leave. Though he'd made it seem as if he was the one doing Mike a favor, he now wore a self-satisfied smile. And Pru began to suspect then that Max hadn't invited her over to his VIP table to just one-up Mike Benz. Rather, he'd been using her to achieve his ultimate goal. Getting Mike Benz to agree to a handshake deal.

This gave Pru pause, because if she was reading the situation right, Max wasn't quite the useless ne'er-do-well he'd come off as in the online gossip blogs. In fact, she'd bet money Cole had no idea what his younger brother was up to.

Her suspicions were confirmed when Max's easygoing smile disappeared as soon as Mike was out of earshot. "Planning to go squealing to my brother about this?" he asked Pru.

Pru answered more frankly than she might have under normal circumstances. "I'm *Sunny's* best friend, not Cole's. I barely see him, and when I do, we're usually not talking hotel business."

"That's not an answer," he pointed out.

Pru lifted her eyebrows. Max was also quite a bit shrewder than she'd originally given him credit for. "Okay…" She set her glass of champagne down and turned toward him on the couch. "Are you saying you don't want me to tell your brother about your plans?"

Max also set aside his glass. "What if I were saying that to you?" he asked.

"Then I'd say if you don't want me to tell him about your hotel, you can just ask me not to, instead of accusing me of being a tattletale."

After giving her an incredulous look, Max said, "Fine, can you *not* tell Cole about this?"

"No problem," Pru answered, somehow managing to

keep her voice light despite the raging headache she could feel coming on. Reacting in an outwardly negative fashion to the club's loud music wasn't exactly in line with the free-spirit party-girl persona she was trying to affect with Max.

"Hey," she said, turning her showgirl smile back on, despite the fact that her head was throbbing. "Want to get out of here?"

Chapter 2

Max didn't want to say he was shocked to be leaving the club with Prudence Washington, but he couldn't exactly say he was not surprised either. He'd already come on to her twice, and he'd been shut down so thoroughly, he hadn't thought he had much of a chance with her.

The first time, she'd listened to his proposal to keep the time-honored tradition of the best man and maid of honor hookup going with a humorless expression on her beautiful face. "No. Just no," she'd answered before walking away from him.

The second time, at Cole and Sunny's shower, he'd decided to try a new tactic, wining and dining Pru before suggesting a sexy rendezvous. But when she saw him approaching, she'd actually turned and walked away before he even had a chance to open his mouth.

However, this time it was Pru who seemed to be coming on to him.

"Do you mind walking?" she asked him with direct eye contact. "My hotel's right down the street."

"Which one?" he asked, testing to see if she was serious about her invitation.

She named a cheap but serviceable hotel brand that he'd heard of in passing but had never stayed at himself.

Her quick reply sent Max's mind into a spin, trying to figure out what had brought on this complete one-eighty. She didn't seem drunk, or even slightly buzzed, despite the amount of alcohol she'd consumed in the hour since she'd shown up in Sin's VIP area. He stepped forward and gave the air between them a surreptitious sniff. She smelled fresh. Simple. Soap, a spritz of perfume and nothing more. Just as she had at Sunny's wedding.

However, Maid of Honor Pru had treated him like a joke—a bad one that she didn't find remotely charming or funny—while this Pru was all sexy invitation.

Tonight, she was dressed in a gold metallic number that he would have bet money was an actual Halston creation. It accented her flawless brown skin in a way that, along with her long, curly extensions, made her look as if she'd time-traveled right out of Studio 54. It was a look he couldn't help but appreciate, especially since the dress's short length showcased her long legs. That was one thing he knew he had in common with his brother. He'd always been a sucker for a nice pair of legs.

And Pru's legs were a match for Sunny's, who had also started out as a Benton showgirl. No surprise there, since all of the women hired to dance for the Benton Revue were required to not only be attractive, but also a minimum height of five foot eight.

In a pair of ruby-red stiletto heels so tall they brought her nearly in line with his height of six feet three inches, Pru looked as if she'd fallen out of an ad for the most idealized version of Las Vegas: beautiful, wild and glossy. Like the kind of girl who could rock your world, and happily keep it a secret.

"What changed?" he asked her straight up. He was good at reading people, and as happy as he was to finally close on this long-withheld deal with Sunny's best friend, he wasn't sure he trusted the terms yet. "You wouldn't give me the time of day in Vegas. And now you're inviting me back to your hotel?"

Pru let his question hang in the air between them for a few seconds, then she stepped forward and whispered low in his ear. "We're not in Las Vegas anymore."

He supposed Pru's comment did explain a few things.

For once, there was no one else present looking on. No Sunny or Cole. Not the kid he vaguely remembered Sunny introducing to him as Pru's younger brother. No one to judge her if she decided to finally take Max up on his original offer to show her a good time.

Good Girl in Las Vegas. Bad Girl in New Orleans. If that was Pru's deal, he thought, he'd definitely take it.

He was already imagining himself taking her out of the little Halston dress. "In that case, let's go back to the hotel where I'm staying. The rooms are bigger."

They ended up having to stop by Pru's hotel on route to his anyway. She had a 5:00 a.m. flight back to Las Vegas and said she needed to grab her bag, so that she could take a taxi from his hotel to the Louis Armstrong once they were done with what she called "our business."

Our business, he thought as he watched her disappear into the hotel. He could already tell that finally sealing the deal on his conquest was going to be fun. A lot of fun.

She emerged from the hotel with a rolling suitcase less than five minutes after going in.

"That was fast."

"I'd already packed," she confessed with a self-deprecating smile. "I thought I'd be at the club longer."

Less than ten minutes later, he was pouring her a glass of wine from a bottle he'd decanted before going out to the Mike Benz gig.

"I'm surprised you're staying at a Lyon Inn," she said. "Isn't there a Benton right up the street?"

She went to stand in front of a watercolor that depicted a historical jazz scene from New Orleans's famous French Quarter. Max joined her there with the two glasses of wine.

He ignored the painting and handed Pru one of the glasses. "I'm not Cole. I don't exclusively stay at Bentons just because they've got my family's name plastered across them."

She took the glass of wine, but her eyes stayed on the watercolor. "But maybe you don't necessarily want people to know you're staying at non-Benton hotels either. Is that why you're staying here under a fake name?"

The front desk staff had greeted him as "Mr. Greer" when he'd entered. Apparently she'd been paying attention.

"One of the reasons," he answered. "My old college roommate, Sorley, is kind of a big deal—in investment circles at least. His investment group owns a stake in this hotel's parent company. But he's kind of a recluse, so sometimes I borrow his name. You know, take it for a spin, so his name won't be too sad about the glamorous life it could be living if it didn't belong to a total bore."

"Also, free hotel room," she said with an amused note in her voice. "Those come in handy when you're used to a certain kind of lifestyle, but no longer have the money to fund it."

He looked over at her. "So you heard about Cole's decision to part ways with the Max Benton brand?"

"Let's just say, the Benton Las Vegas isn't exactly a gossip-free workplace, and I was still working there when you two…uh…parted ways."

"Hmm, no it's not," Max answered. He shrugged. "In any case, it's good to have boring friends in high places."

"I bet," she answered. Her eyes were still on the watercolor. And she still hadn't taken so much as a sip of her wine.

"So tell me about what you've been up to since I saw you last," Max said, trying to draw her attention from the derivative painting and back to him. "Sunny mentioned you'd decided to retire from the line."

Now it was her turn to shrug. "I'm twenty-nine now. Close to retirement age anyway."

There was no official retirement age for Revue girls— mostly because it would have opened the hotel to discrimination lawsuits. But there weren't many showgirls in the line over the age of thirty. "Still, your best friend is married to the Benton CEO. I think you would have got a pass."

"Maybe," Pru answered, her tone vague and distant.

"Tell the truth. You quit because you didn't want to be on the line when Sunny takes over as head choreographer."

From what he'd heard, Sunny was all unicorns and rainbows until you entered one of her dance classes. Then she became a total harridan, on par with a drill sergeant.

That accusation finally drew Pru's brown eyes to him. "That actually is one of the reasons I decided to quit," she admitted with a laugh. "Staying on the line under Sunny probably would have ruined our friendship."

She was pretty when she laughed. More than pretty. It made her sparkle.

Max took the glass out of her hand and set it down along with his on the table underneath the watercolor. "Anything else you want to tell me about yourself, before we move on to 'our business'?"

She raised her eyes to his and said, "No, actually I'm ready to get on with 'our business.'"

Max felt a wolfish smile break out across his face…only to disappear when she pushed away from him and headed not toward the bedroom, but over to the rolling black suitcase she'd left by the door.

She unzipped her bag and pulled out a thick brown legal envelope. "This is for you."

That's when Max realized what this really was. Pru hadn't suddenly changed her mind. It had been a setup from the very beginning.

At first his jaw hardened with knowledge that she'd used his attraction to her to get him exactly where she wanted. But then he decided to school his face into a look of boredom and take the envelope from her.

"What's this?" he asked, undoing the tie closure.

"Not sure," she answered. "Cole didn't go into detail. Just said he wanted it given to you in private."

That explained why she'd accepted the invitation to his room, Max thought with a fresh burst of ire. His brother was nothing if not discreet.

He should have known Cole was behind this. His brother had been trying to get a hold of him ever since Max sent him an email about wanting his trust money paid out in full. He opened the envelope and found a stack of what looked like legal documents, topped off with an eight-by-ten typewritten letter.

Max—

I received your request to have the amount of your trust fund transferred into your bank account, soon after I terminated your payments for serving as the Benton's brand ambassador. While it's true that you're eligible to receive these monies when you turn thirty-five, it's also true that the trust's executor has to sign off on releasing said monies. As you may or may not have realized, now that our grandmother has signed power of attorney over to me, I now serve as your trust's executor. As such, I've decided it's not in your best interest to be given such a large sum of money until you meet the terms we've previously discussed on more than one occasion. Until such time, I will continue to grow your trust with modest investments.

Enclosed, please find a copy of Grandfather's will, along with the terms of your trust.
—Coleridge Benton III

Max immediately balled up the letter and threw it with an angry swing across the room. "That patronizing son of a…" Max let out a violent stream of cuss words. Cole had been nagging him to settle down for years, and now he was using Max's trust to get his way.

Chapter 3

Pru watched with raised eyebrows as Max threw the balled-up letter across the room and swore. The charming playboy who'd brought her to his suite had totally disappeared. What the heck had been in that letter? she wondered, as she watched him pitch it before turning back to her with rage now in his formerly wicked eyes.

Max, she suddenly recalled from her research, hadn't been all fun and games during his years of partying all over the world. He'd actually been arrested a few times for getting in fights. Mostly in other countries, and the Benton lawyers had always gotten the charges dropped. But the fact remained, even though Max Benton officially had a clean record, he'd racked up quite a few charges for engaging in physical violence.

Plus, noses didn't lie, and Max's was crooked with breaks. She took a step back, wondering if she could balance on her ridiculously high heels if it came down to her having to turn tail and run.

"Did you know about this?" he asked, his voice low and dangerous.

"Know about what?" she asked honestly, curious about what would have put him in such a state.

"My brother deciding to play God with my trust fund. His saying I can't have the money from my trust unless I meet his terms."

Well, that sounded like Cole for sure. *Controlling* was one of the first words that came up when making a list of his qualities. And if he had any idea that Max was planning to build his own competing hotel in New Orleans, Pru wasn't at all surprised that he'd decided to play hard-ball. But another part of Pru, who had goals of her own, felt a twinge of guilt. Max most certainly would need his trust money to fulfill his hope of opening his own hotel, and she hated that her assignment had turned out to be of the dream-killing variety.

"What exactly are his terms?" she asked him, licking her lips nervously. "I know you and Cole have some weird history, but maybe you could just meet them," she suggested.

Heaven knew she'd had to do a few pride-killing things when it came to meeting her brother's needs. Like joining the PTA. However, Max didn't strike her as the kind of guy who liked to work too hard to get the money he needed to make things happen. From what she'd read, he'd never actually worked hard for anything in his entire irresponsible life. Why would he start now?

She waited for him to respond with something ridiculous, such as how he was a Benton and therefore *deserved* to just have money handed to him with no strings attached. In her experience, most trust-fund babies had a sense of entitlement the size of Jupiter, and she doubted Max would be any different.

But instead of answering her, Max went completely still, his head inclining as if an idea had suddenly occurred to him.

Then to Pru's surprise, his arm snaked out, pulling her forward, so that her body was flush with his and fully locked into his unexpected embrace.

Pru froze—well, at least the outside of her froze. Another part of her, one that she didn't realize was still in working order after years of celibacy, stirred. Waking up, and to her great embarrassment, actually warming to the sensation of having Max's entire body, including what felt like a rather large erection, pressed against hers.

"So this is what you do now that you've retired from the Revue?" he asked. "Run Cole's blackmail errands."

"No, this was a one-off," she answered, breathless and completely flummoxed. "I'm actually studying to become a PI, and he threw me this case because none of the other people he'd hired to find you had come through. I guess I was sort of his Hail Mary."

Max's eyes narrowed. "Cole sent others, but only you were able to find me," he said. "Why is that?"

Pru shrugged. "I…um…kind of guessed."

"You 'kind of guessed' that I was staying in New Orleans under a pseudonym?"

"Yeah," she answered. "That's kind of my MO. Someone brings me a case to solve, I gather all the information I can, then I just…guess."

"And you guessed I'd be here in New Orleans, using Sorley Greer's name?" he asked.

"No, not exactly. I didn't even know who Sorley Greer was until you mentioned him tonight. But I'd read enough about you to know that you and Mike Benz were friends, and he happened to be doing his first stateside gig tonight. So I flew out here on a hunch."

To her surprise, Max began to chuckle, his chest rumbling against hers. "You flew to New Orleans on a hunch," he repeated. "Because you thought I *might* be in Sin's VIP."

"And I was right. My method worked," she felt compelled to point out.

Max looked down at her, his expression now verging on slightly bemused. "That you were. But I think you might have missed something important in your information-gathering stage, when you came up with your plan to fly out here and trick me into inviting you into my private sanctum."

His observation pulsed in the air between them, filling Pru's chest with a weird combination of dread and anticipation as she asked, "What?"

"You didn't notice in all those stories going around about me that no one's ever said, 'I played Max Benton for a fool, and I totally got away with it.'"

Pru swallowed. He was right. Max did not have a reputation for taking insults lightly.

Her sudden unease at his implied threat must have read on her face.

"Hmm, now you're getting it," he said, his voice almost soft with menace.

Before she could ask what exactly she was supposed to be getting, his mouth found hers in a lazy kiss.

Well…lazy on his part at least. To Pru, it felt like having her insides hollowed out as a pit of long-dormant lust opened up inside her stomach. Max Benton might have been a lot of things—a ne'er-do-well, a brawler, a playboy—but a bad kisser wasn't one of them.

His mouth was confident on top of hers, practically guaranteeing a favorable conclusion for her if she let him keep going.

But she couldn't let that happen. She was a professional. At least she would be after she got her PI license. Professional PIs didn't let themselves get seduced by the people they tracked down.

Just as she was about to rally her mind and body to push him away, he cut off the kiss. So abruptly, that her legs felt a little shaky when he unexpectedly let her go.

Now he was the one who took a step back from her. "You really aren't my brother's flunky?" he asked, his eyes sharp with suspicion.

She bristled, flustered that her body now felt a little bereft, and insulted at the insinuation that she was completely at Cole's beck and call, like one of his servants.

"It's just a case," she answered. "One I was happy to get before I officially become a licensed PI this fall."

He studied her intently, as if he was trying to detect a lie.

She met his gaze straight on, because she wasn't lying, not even by omission this time.

"In that case," Max said, a rather feral smile spreading across his obscenely handsome face, "let's get married."

Chapter 4

Let's get married.

Pru stood there, shocked into silence for what might have been a good minute. Then she said, "What?"

Max folded his arms and leaned against the back of the suite's couch. "You heard me. I said let's get married."

"What?" Pru said again. "No! What the…? Why would you even ask me that? What is wrong with you?"

She didn't wait for his answer, just turned and rezipped her suitcase, grabbing it by the handle as she beat a hasty retreat for the door. Obviously, she had missed something in all her research. Something such as Max Benton being a psycho, one she needed to get away from as soon as possible.

"C'mon," he said, following her out of his suite—or in this case, Sorley Greer's suite. "You're the one who told me to meet my brother's terms, and me getting married— those are his terms."

That announcement surprised her enough to make her stop and turn to face him. "Come again?" she asked.

"Cole wants to put me on a leash and bring me to heel before the Benton Group opens up their first Benton Inn in the fall. This new hotel needs to appeal to regular families, so he's trying to get me to settle down. Like him. That's the real reason he fired me. The real reason I had to sell my shares in the Benton Group to Sorley, so that he wouldn't come after them."

Max shrugged and shook his head as if none of what he was saying was a huge deal. But the fists he'd unconsciously balled at his sides belied his nonchalance. As did his lethal tone.

Pru arched an eyebrow at this latest bit of information about the Benton brothers' relationship. She wasn't one to dispense business advice, especially to someone like Cole Benton, who'd been groomed to be a hotel magnate from a very young age. But despite Max's reputation as a reckless playboy who lived only for fun and clubbing, just an hour with him had revealed to her what her research hadn't.

Max Benton wasn't as devil-may-care as he appeared on paper. No, he was way darker than that. She could practically feel the wolf lurking underneath his surface.

And you couldn't put a wolf on a leash.

If Cole had asked her—he never would have, but if he had—she would have told him to abandon his plan to reel Max in. She didn't have any real evidence to back it up, but she was almost certain that Cole was playing with fire where Max was concerned. Trying to force him into marriage wasn't even a remotely good idea.

"Okay, well that's between you and your brother," she told Max. "I don't want anything to do with that."

He ignored her refusal, regarding her with those pale green eyes of his. "How much is he paying you?"

She shook her head. Funnily enough, when she'd seen the amount Cole was willing to pay someone simply to find Max and deliver a large envelope to him, she'd thought it had been outrageously generous for the service provided. But standing in the hall with Max, she was beginning to think it might not have been enough.

"I'll double it," he said. Then before she could refuse him again, he said, "Tell you what, name your price. Whatever it is, I'll pay it."

She shook her head again, wondering how she'd found herself in such a crazy scenario. "Max," she answered, her voice hard and frank, "there is no amount of money that would convince me to fake marry you."

"Never say never. That's what I always say when it comes to money. You never know when you're going to get hit with a rainy day."

Pru would have thought Max was talking about his own currently diminished circumstances, but his eyes were gleaming at a ten on the wicked-bastard scale. "Don't worry," she answered drily. "I've got a savings account."

If he was insulted by her refusal, it didn't show. He just smirked. "I'd think you'd at least agree to think about it. After doing all that research on me, aren't you a little bit curious?"

"About what?" she asked him. "About how you run through money like water? About how you've been arrested on every continent but Antarctica? About how you got the nickname 'The Ruiner'?" Pru shook her head with her lips turned down. "I'm curious about a lot of things—that comes with being a detective. But not about any of that."

She tilted her suitcase forward. "Now, if you'll excuse me, I'll be heading back to Las Vegas to pick up my check. I'm done here."

He inclined his head to the side and squinted in a way that reminded her of his brother. Though the two men didn't share anything in common but the color of their eyes.

"You sure about that?" he asked her with a smile so lazy, it looked as if he was on the verge of falling asleep. "Because this doesn't feel done, and judging from that kiss, we could have a good time if you fake married me. *A real good time*, as they say here in New Orleans."

Pru swallowed, her body stirring with the memory of how it had felt to have his mouth claim hers, and the reality starlet's words rang in her ears for the second time that night. *Once you go Max, you never go back.*

Okay, time to go, she thought. She turned and walked away from Max Benton as fast as her stiletto heels would allow her.

She had responsibilities to see to back home, she reminded herself. Such as her little brother, whom she'd had to leave alone this weekend in order to fulfill this assignment, and a licensing exam to study for.

"If you change your mind, you know where to find me," Max called behind her. "Just ask for Sorley Greer."

Pru didn't allow herself to stop walking, not until she got to the bank of elevators at the end of the hallway. But as she pushed the down button, she couldn't help looking back to where Max had been standing outside his hotel room door.

He was still there. Watching her with squinted eyes. Watching her as a wolf watches its prey right before it attacks.

Chapter 5

Three weeks later Pru was still shaken by Max's proposal. Not to mention that kiss! So much so that she could barely concentrate on studying for her PI exam. It didn't help that her morning internet scour for everything related to Max Benton had turned up the exact same thing it had every other time she'd searched for news about Max.

Absolutely nothing.

No club spottings from gossip blogs. No wedding announcements either, even though his thirty-fifth birthday was the Friday after next.

Was he really going to give up all that money? If so, how would he continue to fund his lavish lifestyle? Or make his hotel dream come true?

She thought of her recent phone call with her friend who worked at NevadaStar, the Benton Group's official credit union. In a weird continuation of her compulsion to keep looking into Max Benton, she'd decided to follow his money after the fact.

She hadn't during her first instinctual investigation because she knew it was the first thing most detectives did. If none of the other detectives had been able to find him using a money trail, she figured she wouldn't be able to either. But the fact remained that following the money was still one of the best ways to find what someone was up to. And for whatever reason, she could not stop digging into Max Benton's life even though she was no longer getting paid to do so.

Max still hadn't announced a marriage to fulfill Cole's

demands to release his trust money. So maybe, she'd specu-
lated, he had found another source of funding for his hotel.
He was friends with, if not the richest men in the world,
many of their sons and daughters. Including Sorley Greer,
whom Pru had also looked into as a possible financier for
Max's hotel.

However, according to her research, Sorley wouldn't
go for a project this small. He tended toward big investments based on predictions only he seemed to be able to
make. To the point that quite a few other big-time inves-
tors had accused him of insider trading, only to have to
back down from their claims when Sorley's lawyers sent
them strongly worded letters that made generous use of
words such as *defamation* and *libel*. In any case, as good
as Max's hotel idea was, it didn't exactly fit in with the rest
of Sorley's portfolio.

But that didn't mean that Max hadn't found another way
to get the money, which was why she'd asked her friend at
NevadaStar to look into his account. The nice thing about
having been involved in a stage show that aged most of its
pretty participants out at thirty was that she now had contacts working in post–Benton Revue jobs in nearly every
institution in Las Vegas. Very lucky for her, since the truth
was that having contacts in the right places was critical to
working cases as a private investigator.

But this particular lead didn't pan out. According to her
friend, Max hadn't received a single noninterest cent since
Cole cut him off. From the Benton Group or anyone else.
And the interest on his account was seriously measured
in cents now, since he currently had only a three-figure
number left in it.

"I guess stunting like he used to ain't cheap," her friend
observed with a whistle over the youngest Benton heir's
low amount of available funds. "Either he's going to have
to get in back good with his family, or get a real job."

Try as she might, Pru just didn't see Max getting a regu-

lar job. Building a splashy new hotel with his trust money?
Yes. That was the type of big gamble that a guy like Max
would go for. Actually using his marketing degree from
the Boston Institute of Technology in order to earn a paycheck that wasn't a thinly disguised version of his original
allowance? She doubted it.

But maybe he'd just been blustering about starting his
own line of boutique hotels, she thought after finding nary
a mention of Max during her latest internet search. She'd
met guys like Max before back when she'd been into the
Vegas lifestyle. Guys who'd been all talk and no play. Guys
who thought they had what it took to make a big vision
come to life but crapped out before even rolling their dice.

Pru frowned, wishing her fingers weren't itching to call
up her friend at NevadaStar and ask her to go even deeper
with her search. Maybe send over his year-to-date trans-
actions report. Her friend had said most of the money in
his account had gone toward paying credit-card bills. But
maybe there was something she'd missed, something she
hadn't seen.

"Pru?" a voice said behind her.

She turned from the list of Nevada's revised statutes and
limitations that she was supposed to be studying to see her
brother, Jakey, standing in the doorway to her room. He'd
had yet another growth spurt over the summer and now
stood a good five inches taller than her. He'd also been
working out in an effort to relieve the summer boredom, so
he'd also gotten wider over the past two months. The front
of the T-shirt he wore seemed to be crying out for mercy as
it strained against his newly formed muscles, and his old
jogging pants might as well have issued their own flood
warning, they were in such high-water territory.

She screwed up her mouth. "We're going to have to hit
the mall before you leave for your camp next week. Get
you some new clothes."

More money that would have to be spent now that she'd

retired from the Benton Revue and was living off her savings. Luckily, the money Cole had paid her for hunting Max down had nicely cushioned her account. She had enough to not only tide her through until October but also to pay for Jakey's books when he started at UNLV in the fall on a full scholarship.

Buying Jake some more clothes for camp and also a fall wardrobe for college shouldn't be a problem. But still, she worried. She and Jake had been forced to live frugally in the years since their parents' deaths in order to pay rent on an apartment in one of Nevada's best school districts and make ends meet. After Jake got his full scholarship, Pru had thought long and hard before quitting the line in order to pursue what she'd begun to think of as a calling. But she couldn't be sure how soon she'd be able to acquire more work after she got her license. Cases like the one Cole had thrown her didn't come along every day. Plus there would be the costs of renting an office and advertising her services around town.

She needed to watch every penny, she thought. But not at her brother's expense. It wasn't his fault that he kept growing and growing, or that his new health kick upped their weekly grocery bill, or that his going to college came with extra expenses that even having Jakey continue to live at home wouldn't alleviate.

"You know what, let's go to the mall now," she said, glancing at the clock on her bedroom wall. "Maybe we can get some lunch while we're out."

She grabbed her wallet and phone off the desk, slipped them into the back pockets of her bell-bottom jeans and was all set to go. Back in the day before she became Jakey's guardian, she wouldn't have dreamed of leaving the apartment she used to share with her best friend, Sunny, in anything less than full makeup. Back then, even her most casual looks were chosen more to accentuate her assets than for comfort.

But now that she'd retired from the Benton Revue, she'd pretty much stuck to a wardrobe of her mother's old seventies-era clothing throughout the summer. Her mother had been a seamstress along with Sunny's grandmother for the Revue, and she'd taken excellent care of even her most casual clothes. True, seventies and early eighties vintage wasn't the most glamorous look, but wearing these clothes made Pru feel closer to her mother, even though she was no longer here.

"Actually," said Jake with an apologetic wince, "I was hoping maybe we could go down to the storage unit and do some upkeep on Dad's car."

"Oh…sure," Pru said, quickly resetting.

About twenty minutes later, they were pulling the cover off their dad's black '55 Thunderbird.

Back when they'd been forced to downsize in order to keep Jakey in his school district, Pru had paid for storage space and an additional garage unit for their dad's Thunderbird. He'd inherited the car from his own father, and Pru had grown to highly value it. Not just because it was a much sought-after collectible, but also because it was Jakey's unspoken inheritance. Their happy and healthy parents hadn't been prescient enough to take out a life insurance policy, but her father had left this car behind. And that was why Pru had remained diligent about its upkeep all these years. She made sure that she and Jakey did the necessary work to guarantee the car would stay in good enough shape for Jakey to drive it someday.

However, this particular trip wasn't really about their father's Thunderbird. Asking her if they could go down to the garage unit to do some upkeep on their dad's car was Jakey's way of telling her he needed to talk. Over the years she'd been his guardian, she'd guided him through first dates, first breakups, major disappointments and lost friendships over the hood of that car.

"So what's up?" she asked Jakey as he lifted up the Thunderbird's hood.

"I dunno," Jakey mumbled. He fiddled with the oil cap for a few seconds, then he said, "It's stupid."

"Okay, maybe," Pru answered. "Tell me anyway."

More fiddling. "I don't even know why I'm bringing it up. It's not going to happen. I know it's not going to happen."

Despite her increasing curiosity, Pru casually walked over to get the motor oil from a nearby shelf. "You know I don't believe in 'not going to happen.' Not when it comes to you. I'm your big sis, remember?" She handed the motor oil to him. "Whatever you need, just tell me, and I'll figure it out. I always do."

"Yeah, I know you do, but…" He trailed off. "You know what? Never mind. Let's just finish this and go to the mall."

He reached to take the motor oil from her, but she held on to it, refusing to let it go.

"No, tell me, Jakey," she insisted, dropping all pretense of feeling casual about this conversation. "Are you in trouble?" she asked, real alarm flaring up inside her. "Whatever it is, I'll figure it out, I promise you. Just tell me."

"No, I'm not in trouble!" he said, rushing to reassure her. "It's more a good thing…I guess. An opportunity. I… um…got off the wait list to BIT."

Pru's eyebrows rose nearly to her hairline, her first thoughts going to Max, who'd received and wasted a degree in marketing from BIT. "BIT? You mean like the Boston Institute of Technology? That BIT?"

"Yeah, that BIT," Jakey answered with a sheepish smile.

"Oh my gosh, Jakey! That's wonderful!" She put aside the motor oil and hugged him. "I didn't even know you applied there! That wasn't on the list you showed me!"

"Yeah, I didn't want you to waste your money," he said. "So I used some of the money Aunt Sunny gave me for Christmas to pay the application fee, and I got wait-listed.

But I guess they must have decided to take me off the wait list because I got an email that I was in two weeks ago."

"Two weeks ago?" Pru repeated, her mouth dropping open. "And you're just now telling me?"

Jakey shrugged. "It's not like I can go. They gave me a financial-aid package, but it's not a full deal like UNLV. It also doesn't cover room and board or books or the flight out there. There's no way you could afford it. It was stupid of me to even apply. It's just… Dad used to talk about me going there, and I already know I want to become an engineer. I thought I should at least try to get in. For him."

Pru completely understood. Her parents had both come from poor backgrounds and her father had used education as a means to break through to the middle class, earning his degree and becoming a high school math teacher. He'd carried big hopes and dreams for Jakey not just following in his footsteps but going even further than he did. He would have considered Jakey getting into a big math-and-science school such as BIT a dream come true.

"Dad would have been so proud of you," she told him, her eyes going soft with fond memories of their father. "You're going to BIT."

He shook his head. "It's too much money."

"How much?"

"Too much?"

"Just tell me how much, Jakey."

So he did, and the number made Pru a little breathless. That was over five times what she currently had tucked away in savings for Jakey's continued education.

But still she said, "You're going to BIT."

Jakey shook his head again. "There's no way you can get that much money together before the school year starts. I was thinking maybe we could ask Aunt Sunny, but Dad was always saying…"

"…remember what 'make ends meet' really means," she finished for him.

Their father had grown up in Vegas and seen too many friends from his old neighborhood succumb to both credit and gambling debts. He hadn't believed in buying anything on credit, not even cars. Back in the day, Pru hadn't dared ask her father for money—even when she'd blown through her entire paycheck with more than a week to go until she got paid again. It just wasn't worth receiving one of their father's long "neither a beggar nor a borrower be" lectures.

Jakey was right. Besides, there was no way she could pay Sunny that amount back, even if she was willing to borrow as opposed to work for money. She'd have to find another way to get the money. One that wouldn't involve a huge debt load on her part. But how?

The answer hit her with a sickening thud, crashing all the way down to the bottom of her stomach.

Never say never. That's what I always say when it comes to money. You never know when you're going to get hit with a rainy day.

"Pru? Pru?" her brother said.

Pru blinked.

"Are you okay? You just went real quiet."

"Yeah, sure. Better than okay." She pasted on a smile for her brother's sake. "I'm just wondering if they'll be selling winter coats at the mall yet. You'll need one for Boston."

Jakey's whole face lit up with a goofy smile. "Probably not. We should probably just concentrate on getting a few things for camp and order the coat online."

"That's a great idea. Do you…um, mind if I go make a phone call while you finish this up? I've got a possible client I need to touch base with. Then we'll go to the mall."

"And maybe we can call Aunt Sunny up to celebrate me getting into BIT tonight?" he suggested. "Maybe Cole, too."

Thanks to their mutual interest in cars, Cole and Jakey had become buddies since the CEO had been with Sunny.

"Sunny's still teaching her summer class in New York," Pru answered apologetically. "And Sunny says Cole's been clocking extra hours, training some new vice president, so that he'll be good to go before he goes on paternity leave in the fall."

Thank goodness, she silently added to herself. Even if Sunny and Cole weren't otherwise occupied, she doubted she could have looked either of them in the eye—not considering what she was about to agree to.

"But we'll go wherever you want tonight," she told Jakey. "Just name the place."

She took out her phone and waved as she walked away from him, as if everything was terrific. Because things were terrific. Her brother would be going to his dream college in Boston. And she'd make it happen, because it was no less than what he'd deserved. He'd lost his parents at a tender age, and he deserved to be happy. He deserved to get everything he'd ever dreamed of, and she would make sure he got it.

Even if she had to make a deal with the devil in order to do so.

"Looks like there *is* an amount of money that would get you to fake marry me," was the first thing Max said after she told him what it would take for her to agree to marry him.

Despite his words, he didn't seem surprised at all, not when he answered the phone, not even when she'd answered his greeting with a five-figure dollar amount. A chill ran down Pru's back. It had been easy to get Max on the phone. Easier than she'd thought it would be. The front desk at the Lyon had put her right through as soon as she gave them her name, and Max had picked up on the first ring, as if he'd been expecting her call.

"What changed?" he asked, his voice laced with lazy amusement.

"My brother got into BIT," Pru answered through gritted teeth.

Max whistled. "My alma mater! Nice! I think I remember maybe going to one or two classes while I was there."

Yet, he had graduated with a degree, *Which he never even bothered to use*, Pru thought, shaking her head. Apparently, if your family donated enough money to your college, it was enough to earn even the most shiftless student the degree of his choice.

"Do we have a deal or what?" Pru asked.

It occurred to her then that Max could simply be toying with her from the other side of the phone now. He might have no intention of honoring his brother's terms. Or even more likely, he could have found someone way more appropriate to fulfill them.

Pru's shoulders tightened at the thought of Max rescinding his original offer.

"Look, if you've already found someone else, just let me know now," she told Max. "This might be fun and games for you. But it's my brother's future we're talking about, so if you're not serious—"

"Oh, I'm serious, Prudence," he said, his voice suddenly a lot darker on the other side of the phone. "You have no idea."

Another chill ran down Prudence's back. Again, she got the sense that there was more to Max than what he was showing the world. Something lurking inside him. Something that would come up and bite her if she weren't careful.

But she had to do this. For her brother. She'd do whatever it took to make his dreams come true.

So she pressed forward and pretended to be much braver than she actually felt. "If you're really serious, stop toying with me. Do we have a deal or what?"

A long moment of silence passed. "Yes, Pru, we have a deal."

She swallowed, barely able to believe that he was still open to marrying her, or that she was really going to go along with his scheme. "Okay, then, I guess I should ask when and where and how long?"

She could practically feel Max smiling through the phone. Smiling like a wolf.

Chapter 6

When? Pretty soon as it turned out. Saturday to be exact, just six days before Max Benton's thirty-fifth birthday. Apparently that was how long Max's non-Benton family lawyers needed to produce the kind of prenup they were going to need for such an unorthodox arrangement. One that allowed them both to get a quickie divorce under already-agreed-upon terms as soon as his trust fund check cleared the bank.

Pru was initially happy for the short reprieve. But the days seemed to fly by in a haze of dread that didn't allow her to get in much quality study time. Before she was nearly ready, the day of her wedding had arrived, casting an ominous shadow over everything she did from the moment she woke up.

At least she didn't have to figure out what to do with Jakey while she was dealing with Max. The morning before their wedding, Pru drove her brother to Henderson for the Focus Leadership Camp. Jakey had been attending the two-week program dedicated to teaching underprivileged youth leadership skills since the age of thirteen, and he'd been looking forward to volunteering as a counselor all summer.

However, as they drove to Henderson, he fiddled with the passenger-door lock on Pru's tiny hatchback. "Maybe I should stay in Vegas," he said. "Try to get a job."

"No," Pru answered before the sentence was fully out of his mouth. Even if Jakey hadn't been looking forward to this all summer, she didn't want him anywhere near Vegas tonight.

After a bunch of back-and-forth, Pru shut down all of Jakey's arguments by simply dropping him off at his destination. She got his duffel out of the back and just about tossed it at him, then gave him a quick hug and sped off before he could protest any further.

She got home in record time, ate lunch and tried to use the hours before her wedding event to study. But she gave up on that around dinnertime.

How was she supposed to think about anything else, other than the fact that she would soon be marrying Max Benton? Tonight. For money.

Her stomach churned and Pru decided against warming up the takeout she and Jake had ordered the previous night. The only thing worse than marrying Max Benton would be throwing up in the middle of the ceremony.

A knock sounded on the door about an hour before she'd planned to leave to meet up with Max at the Benton.

She frowned. The complex was gated and no one was supposed to be able to get in unless she buzzed them through.

But sure enough, there was a large Latino man in her doorway. One she recognized as Cole's driver.

"Tomas?" she said, opening the door. "What are you doing here?"

He gave her an apologetic smile. "Sorry to bother you. Mr. Max must not have told you I was coming."

Actually, she hadn't heard from Mr. Max, other than an email informing her they'd be getting married at the Benton at the rather late hour of 10:00 p.m. The lack of communication had been just one of the reasons she'd been so jumpy over the past few days, and she was beginning to wonder if he'd be a no-show since she couldn't be sure if he was even in town.

This could all be some kind of elaborate joke on his part,

she'd thought a few times over the course of the past few gloomy days. An act of revenge for playing him for a fool when she'd delivered his brother's envelope. Pru had sent her brother to school with rich kids long enough to know they could be cruel, especially to those who didn't have the resources to defend themselves.

But if Tomas was any indication, Max was not only in town, but availing himself of Cole's driver.

"He shouldn't have bothered you," Pru said, embarrassed to have someone she knew and liked entangled in all of this. "I could have driven myself."

"No bother at all," Tomas answered. "Besides, he wanted to make sure you got your wedding outfit in time to change before we got to the Benton."

He held up a dress bag.

And Pru's heart sank, knowing on instinct that the wedding dress Max had chosen for her was probably nothing like the simple white crochet dress she'd been planning to wear for their farce of a wedding.

Fifteen minutes later, she stared at herself in the mirror, completely aghast. Apparently, Max liked vintage, too. In fact, he had sent over one of the Benton Revue's original showgirl costumes, a scoop-neck top and bottom, covered in silver trim, all held together by a netted stocking.

It came with a huge white feather headdress and matching white bustle, which thankfully fanned over and completely covered her backside. And the rhinestones and silver trimming shone so bright, the costume might well have been mistaken for white. But other than that, it looked nothing remotely like a wedding dress.

After a full moment of staring at her image in horror, she decided to just throw a long cardigan over the ostentatious number and leave before she could think too hard about what she was doing. She comforted herself with the fact that the old-timey costumes didn't expose nearly as much skin as the current crop of Benton Revue getups.

She and Sunny had never been among the girls who danced topless, but their barely there bikinis, dripping with fake jewels, hadn't been designed to leave much to the tourists' imaginations.

Still, there was a difference between dancing in a revue with two dozen other girls and walking across the lobby of the Benton in an old showgirl costume beside Tomas. The driver's large body blocked out a lot of the stares, but not nearly all of them, and Pru's cheeks burned as they made their way through the Benton.

She was a little surprised when Tomas passed by the bank of elevators in the main lobby. Since Benton Girls got a steep discount, she'd been to quite a few ceremonies at the Benton and knew that most of their wedding salons were upstairs.

But Tomas kept on going, past more staring tourists and hotel employees. So she guessed that meant they would be getting married in the Benton ballroom, which she supposed wasn't that big of a surprise since that was where Sunny and Cole had gotten married. Still, the thought of getting married in the same place as her best friend felt a bit like sacrilege. Sunny and Cole had married for love, whereas she and Max were doing this for much, much different reasons. She whispered a silent apology to her best friend, hoping Sunny wouldn't hold this against her after it was all said and done.

But when Tomas finally stopped walking, it was in front of the towering double doors to the Benton's main nightclub. This particular nightclub was known as one of Vegas's premiere hotspots. It was the place to go Thursday through Saturday night if you wanted to play a game of Spot the Celebrity. And like many clubs in Vegas, it had a one-word title. In this case, one meant to convey a sense of decadent luxury and wicked-good times.

MAX was written in huge red letters across the top of the doors.

Pru's heart sank. She used to come here all the time before her parents died, but not once after she'd taken over as Jakey's guardian. She remembered now the other showgirls talking about how the club had been closed for a much-needed update and then reopened under a brand-new name.

Apparently, that brand-new name had been Max. Pru let go an irritated sigh. Of course this was where Max had decided to hold their wedding ceremony.

"Son of a…" Pru said, covering her heavily made-up eyes with one hand.

When she uncovered them, she found Tomas looking down at her sympathetically. "You sure you're ready for this?" he asked her.

No, she wasn't. She definitely, definitely wasn't ready for any of this.

But she took off her cardigan and handed it to Tomas anyway.

The next morning Pru woke inside a cloud of white. Everything was white and soft, and for a moment she thought she might have gone to heaven.

But then she lifted her head and realized that though nearly everything in the room was white, this was not heaven. No, definitely not heaven, she thought squinting against the too-bright sun streaming through two wall-to-wall, floor-to-ceiling windows. After her eyes adjusted, she realized she was in a hotel room, one she vaguely recognized from pictures she'd seen in brochures as one of the Benton's panoramic corner suites.

Her head was throbbing, her mouth dry to the bone from lack of hydration. And, she noticed the bed wasn't all white. There was brown and black makeup all over her pillow. She'd slept in her makeup? That was so bad for your skin. Like most showgirls, she never did that. She sat up in bed, wondering what the heck had happened to her last night only to realize that she wasn't wearing anything.

That's when memories from the previous night came bursting back through all the cotton wool inside her head.

Her entering the nightclub to the loud, raucous cheers of what had to be at least a thousand of Max's "closest friends."

The flash of paparazzi taking pictures as she made her way over to Max, who was standing on top of the stage normally reserved for DJs and wearing a skinny white tuxedo. Him pulling her up to join him with a devilish grin.

Max handing her a shot glass with some kind of blue liquid inside as he whispered in her ear, "This is how Max Benton would get married, so play along, Prudence."

Her taking the shot, actually grateful for it, because she knew she would need to be severely altered to go through with this.

The images flashed by quicker after that. Her and Max signing the official prenup in front of the cheering crowd. Her and Max taking a shot for every vow exchanged.

There had been dancing after that. A lot of it, with Max in the middle of the throbbing throng. She remembered laughing with him, and feeling free. Freer than she had in a very long time.

But what had happened after that? She sat up and frantically looked around, trying to figure out how she'd gone from dancing with Max Benton to waking up in one of the bridal suites.

"I see you're finally awake."

She turned to see Max walking into the room, looking fresh as a daisy, his freshly washed black hair in a stubby knot on top of his head. Wearing nothing but a towel…and a titanium wedding ring on his left hand.

Despite the circumstances, Pru couldn't help but stare. Max Benton, as it turned out, didn't spend all his time in the club. He must have also been clocking some serious hours at the gym, too, because he was cut from head to toe with lean muscles. The sight of his nearly naked body was so impressive that Pru couldn't take her eyes off it for a long entranced second before it occurred to her why he was staring back with an equally impressed look on his face.

Then she remembered she was sitting there still naked as the day she'd been born.

With a gasp, she grabbed the white duvet, bringing it up to cover her chest before demanding, "What happened last night? Tell me. *Now.*"

Chapter 7

Prudence had warned Max she'd no longer be there when they woke up.

"Wanna do me?" she'd asked him when she'd crawled onto the bed in her showgirl costume. "I'm only here for one night."

Max, who had a rule about sleeping with a completely wasted woman, had answered, "I don't think so, sweetheart."

Then he'd come over to the bed, undid her feather bustle and started the surprisingly complicated process of getting her showgirl costume unzipped, unhooked and off her body. The idea had been to get her out of the costume and tucked into bed, but Pru didn't make it easy for him. She was little to no help, forcing him to turn her body every which way in order to get her undressed.

And then there'd been the big reveal of her fully naked body. As it turned out, Pru had a body built for loving: soft wide hips, a heart-shaped backside and a set of breasts so glorious, they made his mouth water at the thought of tasting their black-cherry centers.

"You sure you don't want to keep the party going?" she'd asked, arching her back and extending her long legs in a classic pinup-girl pose.

Max had gritted his teeth before reaching for the duvet and yanking it, so that she came tumbling out of her sexy pose.

By the time she recovered, he was holding up the duvet, letting her know that he was ready for her to stop tempting him and lie down. He *needed* to cover the sight of her nearly irresistible body with the blanket.

Pru obediently lay down, but she continued to argue with him. "C'mon, Max, don't be like that. I had so much fun tonight." She pouted. "Just do me, okay? One time. That's all I'm asking."

It was a hard argument to resist. Especially with Pru running her hands over her body, making it blatantly obvious that she would rather have him on top of her than the blanket he was holding.

But Max, who prided himself on not living by the rules, followed this particular rule of consent for good reason.

He averted his eyes from her delectable body and reminded himself why. *It's a good way to get taken to court*, he told himself. *Do you really want to be that douche bag who gets a girl drunk in order to get her into bed?* he'd asked himself.

No, he didn't want to be that guy, but he did want Pru. There was that unfinished business in New Orleans that they had. The kiss that had continued to haunt him in the weeks before she'd called to accept his offer. And he still owed her for using her womanly wiles to basically serve him with his brother's stupid demands.

But he didn't want Pru like this. Not in some drunken lay, meant to cap off a night of partying it up. No, he decided, when he took Pru, he wanted her completely sober. He wanted her to give in to him, not because she was drunk, but because she wanted him, wanted the things he could and would do to her body.

Determined to do this his way, he moved in with the blanket. But at the last moment, she grabbed one of his hands with two of hers, bringing it down to rest on one perfect globe.

"Max Benton, do you know how hot you are?" she asked him.

Max went still. He could feel her heavily beaded nipple

against his palm, and Max's cock jumped inside his white tuxedo pants in response.

Perhaps sensing that Max was at the edge of his restraint, Pru let out a sexy moan before asking, "Do you have any idea how hot you made me when we were dancing together? I want you so bad right now, Max. Please."

For a moment, Max was paralyzed with lust, locked in a battle with himself to throw his number-one rule straight out the window.

Pru totally took advantage of that. Her hand snaked around the back of his neck and pulled his head down to hers for a kiss so hot, it made his entire body pound with need. His instincts howled to take what she was offering.

But he somehow managed to pull back. He tore his lips away from hers and said, "Pru, I want to. You have no idea how much I want you. But not like this, okay? Not when you've had too much to drink."

He cursed himself now for letting that happen. When he started offering her shots, he'd thought she'd do the same thing she'd obviously done in New Orleans—pour them out when he wasn't looking.

He'd used a trick one of the old Benton magicians had taught him back in the day for making drinks disappear in front of a large audience, while Pru knocked back every shot during the vows and then grabbed a bottle of champagne for all the photo ops Max had prearranged for after their stunt ceremony.

At first, Max had thought Pru was just playing her part to the tee. Pretending to be an anything-goes party girl like in New Orleans. But when the photos were done and they were free to do their own thing, instead of running to Tomas so that he could drive her home, she'd pulled Max out onto the dance floor.

Some showgirls he'd met, even the ones with dance degrees, weren't particularly great dancers when it came to getting out on the floor at a nightclub. Sometimes they were stiff when they didn't have choreographed moves to follow, or more interested in how they looked while dancing than actually having fun.

Pru wasn't one of those girls. She'd dragged Max away from the cameras into the middle of the crowd because according to her that was the absolute best place to be. Then she'd danced with him. Really danced. Abandoning herself to the music and using him as an instrument of her appreciation, until eventually it felt as if they were one body, writhing together on the dance floor, held in thrall to the music's sway. They danced like this for what felt like hours, him reveling in the feel of holding her close as they moved in time with the fast music.

When Max had sent Tomas home and arranged for the hotel room, his intentions had been honorable—sort of. Let Pru sleep off the night's excesses, then continue the party in the morning.

After the night they'd had, he'd doubted Pru would have much more energy than what it would take to climb into bed. He hadn't counted on her propositioning him, or making it so hard for him to turn her down.

But he did it. He ended the kiss before it got out of control.

"Not tonight," he told her, bringing his hand up from her breast and using it to cup her face instead. She was still beautiful, he couldn't help but notice, even with her eye makeup all smudged and her long curly hair looking less than perfect.

"Tomorrow, I'll make you feel good, give you everything you want, I promise. Just wait until morning, sweetheart. We'll spend the whole day in bed."

She smiled at him, her eyes hooded with desire. "That sounds really nice," she said. "I wish I could."

"Why can't you?" he asked. "Whatever you've got planned, cancel it. We'll keep the party going, just like you said."

"I wish we could keep the party going forever," she whispered. Then her smile turned sad. "But we can't. I won't be here tomorrow morning. If you want me, this is your last chance, your only chance."

Max had frowned the night before, not understanding. But instead of answering his follow-up questions, Prudence had turned over and fallen asleep without any further discussion. Leaving Max to sleep on the couch because he didn't trust himself to occupy the same bed as Pru or her naked, nubile body.

He'd taken a cold shower before going to sleep. Then another one after waking up from an erotic dream involving him stripping Pru out of a real wedding dress and taking her from behind before the dress had even hit the floor.

He'd taken the second shower in the hopes of calming himself down a bit before he woke Pru up to fulfill the promise he'd made her the previous night. He didn't want their first time together to be over in a few blazing minutes.

But when he came out of the shower, it hadn't been necessary to rouse his sleeping bride, because she was already awake. With her long hair in a tangle of curls, and naked, she looked every bit as enticing as she had the night before.

She stared at him in his towel, her dark brown eyes lighting with appreciation, which had given him momentary hope that what Pru had said last night hadn't been a case of drunken gibberish.

But then a look of horror had overtaken her face as she covered her breasts with the duvet and demanded to know what had happened last night. Her face accusing, as if he hadn't used every weapon in his willpower arsenal to keep his hands off her.

That was when he understood exactly what Pru had meant the night before. Wedding Night Pru, the woman who'd met every challenge he'd put to her, the woman who had posed and laughed and talked and danced with him all night, the woman who had kissed him as he'd never been kissed before—she was gone.

Gone and replaced with the tight-faced would-be detective currently clutching the duvet as if he'd done something indefensible to her.

"Don't worry, sweetheart. If we had hooked up last night, you'd have no doubt about what had happened, because you would be feeling it this morning. All over your body."

His words hit their mark, and even though Pru's face was too dark to show a blush, he got to enjoy the show of her looking away from him, obviously flustered.

But his enjoyment was brought up short when she said, "I have to go. I have to get home."

"Why?" he asked. "Your brother's at camp. What else do you have to do today?"

She turned on him, her eyes sharp. "How did you know my brother was at camp?" she asked.

He gave her a lazy shrug and took a seat on the suite's dark gray couch. "I guess the same way you knew to look for me at the club in New Orleans. Research."

She wrinkled her nose, obviously not liking the idea of someone prying into her life as she'd pried into his. "So yeah, I need to go. Like right now."

She got out of bed, taking the covers with her, but stopped short when she saw the showgirl outfit on the ground. "You left vintage clothing lying around on the floor?" she nearly shrieked, as if this, and not waking up in his bed, was the most horrific thing she'd experienced that morning.

Supposing he should be grateful to have waking up in his bed pushed into second place, he watched her perform the rather impressive task of keeping the heavy duvet in place as she picked up the old costume. She draped it across her two arms and carried it like a wounded animal over to the suite's large walk-in closet.

"You should ask whoever pulled this for you to come up and get it," she said as she disappeared into the closet. "Make sure it gets properly cleaned and put back wherever you found it…"

She suddenly popped her head out of the closet and asked, "Where exactly did you find it?"

Max didn't reply, knowing she probably wouldn't like the answer.

But his refusal must have been clue enough, because she groaned. "Tell me—please tell me—you did not pull a costume from Nora Benton's special collection."

"My grandmother loves weddings, and if she'd been here to ask, she would have been happy to loan it to you."

That was true. His Irish grandmother had been a Benton Revue girl herself. She would have been thrilled to see one of her costumes make an appearance at her grandson's wedding—crazy but true, she was that kind of grandmother.

However, it was also true that he'd have hell to pay from his redheaded grandmother when she got back from her European vacation at the end of the summer. It was one thing to get married without inviting her or Cole. It was another to do so with this particular bride. A girl she liked so much, that she'd actually cheered when Pru turned him down at his brother's wedding, with a "Thatta girl, Pru" before telling her own grandson, "She's too good for the likes of you."

"So you have a thing for vintage," he said before Pru could argue with him any further about the costume. "Is that because your mom did costume work for the line?"

"Yes, that's exactly why," Pru answered. She emerged from the closet, now dressed in one of the suite's complimentary white robes. "And she'd be rolling over in her grave if she knew you'd thrown an original Benton Revue costume on the floor."

She cinched the robe's belt tighter around her waist and asked, "Can you call Tomas? Tell him to meet me in the garage? Sunny gave me the code to Cole's private elevator, so I can take it and meet him down there."

He answered her furtive request with a cool look. "Depends."

"Depends on what?" she asked, annoyance etched across her face.

"On where you put the girl I met last night," he answered. "You're holding her hostage, and I'm not letting you leave here until you tell me how to get her back."

"G-get her back?" Pru blinked at Max, everything inside her cringing up.

This is why she worked so hard to keep the girl she used to be completely suppressed. The old Pru had never been anything but trouble—a walking invitation for regrets.

Pru cursed herself. Yeah, she'd been understandably nervous about getting married in front of a nightclub packed with Max's friends, but she never should have drank so much. Never should have risked letting her out.

Pru took a breath and answered as calmly as she could, "Max, I drank a lot last night. I probably said some things I shouldn't have." Her cheeks heated. "Probably did some things I shouldn't have, too. But it was because I was drunk. That girl last night wasn't me."

"I don't believe you."

Four words. Said quietly, but with more conviction than she would have guessed Max Benton capable of.

She opened her mouth to once again feint what he had guessed correctly. To once again try to convince him that she didn't have a wild party girl trapped inside her, one she'd been ruthlessly suppressing for the past five years.

But she was saved from doing so by the sound of a vibrating ring. It was Max's smartphone, going off on the little table beside the couch.

He picked it up and smirked. "It's my brother," he told her before answering the phone with a fake-chummy, "Cole, bro. What's up?"

Cole answered and Max's smirk grew even more pronounced. "Well, you know me, bro. *Impetuous* is my middle name. Sorry you had to hear about it on the news, but Pru's a great girl. You know that. I'm just happy she agreed to marry me, so of course I wanted to lock that down sooner rather than later."

Max nodded, looking bored, as he remained silent. "Okay, duly noted. You and Sunny want to be invited the next time Pru and I get married. We'll keep that in mind. Meanwhile, should I pick up my trust-fund check from your office or do you just want to transfer the funds straight into my account?"

Cole answered again, and this time the smirk fell off Max's face. In fact the more Cole talked, the more furious Max looked.

But in the end, all Max said was, "Fine. See you later."

Then he hung up, his jaw ticking.

"What did he say?" Pru asked, her curiosity temporarily superseding her need to run from the room. "Is he refusing to give you the money again, even though you met his terms?"

"No," Max answered, his voice tight. "He says he'll sign off, but he has one more condition. He wants me to come meet him to fill out the paperwork."

"That's not a bad condition," Pru told him. "You can do that. Isn't his office right upstairs on the thirty-fifth floor?"

Max rubbed a hand over his face, suddenly seeming weary beyond his years. "Yes it is. But he's not there today. He's in Utah, on the company's annual executive retreat near the Grand Staircase."

Pru would have argued that this wasn't so bad either.

The Grand Staircase was only a few hours' drive away. If Max left now, he could get there before lunch maybe.

But then Max let the other shoe drop. "He wants me to come meet him in Utah. And he wants me to bring you."

Chapter 8

Pru hadn't loved the idea of being married to Max, and she was even less enthusiastic about having to pretend to be in love with him directly to his brother's face.

Max knew this because she'd made him wait outside in his Ferrari sports car when he dropped her off at her apartment to get a shower and put on something to wear for the short trip to the Sinclair Lodge, a retreat a few miles from Utah's Grand Staircase–Escalante National Monument. The shower and change of clothes didn't seem to help her mood. She barely said a word in the car ride up to Utah, not even when he baited her with questions about Wedding Night Pru.

She maintained her hostile silence, breaking it only to greet the Sinclair Lodge's manager, who handed Max a set of old-fashioned metal keys and guided them to their room on the second floor. The manager walked beside Pru up the stairs, telling her about the lodge's history. How it had started out as a private residence for the Sinclairs, a prominent Pittsburgh steel family, but had later been converted into a corporate retreat by Andrew Sinclair, the youngest Sinclair brother, who had decided to leave behind the steel business and start his own line of specialized hotels. Ski resorts, dude ranches and retreats such as this one, which were rented out only to large groups for reunions, corporate retreats, etc.

Max only half listened to the manager's explanation. Instead he remembered how he'd partied a few times with Nathan Sinclair, the older, much less upstanding of the Sinclair brothers, back before he'd decided to take over Sinclair Steel and become boring. Like Cole. Pru, on the other hand, was as curious about this as she seemed to be about most things, asking the manager several follow-up questions about the lodge and its amenities. He supposed that curiosity was part of what made her a natural detective.

However, after the manager left them alone, she barely glanced at the large rustic room, which they'd been told was one of the only rooms that had its own bathroom. One Max quickly availed himself of after the long drive.

When he came back out to the bedroom, she was still standing near the door, her arms crossed over the peach swing top she'd changed into, along with a denim pencil skirt. He noted that she had slipped the large diamond he'd given her at their nightclub ceremony onto her left ring finger. But he also noted that she was standing at the door, about as far away from the bed in the center of the room as she could possibly get.

"All right, let's get this over with," she said, uncrossing her arms.

Max, too, was eager to get the business with his brother done with, so he could get around to properly celebrating with Pru.

However, if the way Pru's shoulders stiffened when he strung his arm around them outside their room was any indication, she had no intention of letting him get anywhere near her tonight.

"Look, this is important to me, sweetheart," he reminded her. "You want your brother at BIT, so it's time to play your part."

Pru's shoulders relaxed a little. But not much. "You're not playing your part so great either."

He gave her a quizzical look. "What do you mean? Anybody who saw us right now would think I was into you."

Pru stopped and shrugged off his arm before turning to face him. "No, they'd think you want to hook up with me, because *this* isn't how a guy looks at a woman he's seriously into…"

She schooled her face into a surprisingly dead-on impression of Max's smirk, complete with his patented wicked gleam. Then she said, "*This* is how people look at each other when they're really in love."

He expected her to peg him with a simpering gaze, filled with longing—the kind that women who claimed to be in love with him had worn. The kind of gaze that had let him know in the past when it was time to let go of the current girl he was with and move on to the next one.

But Pru didn't gaze at him like that. Instead she looked at him. Just looked at him, her eyes clear and calm, with a soft twinkle in them.

She was right. This look was nothing like the one that had come before it. He'd taken a few fists in the stomach before, and this look felt exactly like that. A total gut punch.

"Where did you learn to do that?" he asked her.

She let the expression slip from her face. "My parents were the real deal. I remember how they used to look at each other. Plus when I was just an amateur detective, showgirls with possibly cheating boyfriends were like seventy percent of my cases, I had to learn to tell the difference."

She laughed, mistaking his stricken expression for performance fear. "Don't worry. You can do it. Just don't think about it as giving me a fake lovey-dovey look. Focus on not sounding smug when you talk to me. And when you look at me, *really* look at me."

Max laughed and Pru's face lit up. "Exactly," she said. "When you look at me, just kind of laugh. But sincerely and on the inside. Got that?"

Max did get it. He looked down at her with the same soft twinkle in his eyes, wondering if she had any idea how pretty she was when she smiled up at him like this.

"Max! Pru!"

They both looked up to see Cole now standing outside the doorway of his room, which as it turned out was located directly down the hallway from theirs. Close enough for Max to see his older brother clearly now, but not close enough that Cole could have possibly heard what they were talking about. So to Cole, Max and Pru might actually have looked like what they were only pretending to be.

Two people, totally and unexpectedly in love.

"Sunny told me on the phone this morning that you and Pru made sense, and it looks like she was right. For once, you chose well, Max. I very much approve."

Max had to work hard to keep his eyes from rolling. Judging from the self-congratulatory smirk on Cole's face as they all sat down together in his master suite's small seating area, Cole had fallen for their act, hook, line and sinker.

"Congratulations, you two," he said after they were all seated, Pru and Max on the couch and him in a wingback chair made of cowhide.

Cole's eyes floated to Pru's wedding ring, on full display, since she was resting her left hand on top of Max's right, which he'd placed on her knee. "That wedding was…a little unorthodox." Cole took a moment to shoot Max a censorious look before apparently deciding to get over it. "But I'm sure we'll be able to spin your wedding into a nice bit of publicity when we launch the Benton Inn this fall. The Benton Playboy finally settles down. End of an era."

"Okay, sure we can do that," Max said, waiting for the other shoe to drop. Cole was being polite, which naturally made Max suspicious, since everything was a chess game in Cole's world. He never made a move without another one in mind.

"But before we sign the trust paperwork, I wanted to ask if you'd be open to a partial payout."

And there it was. Cole playing the part of the controlling big brother again.

"No," Max answered. "I'd like my money. All of it. Now."

The expression on Cole's face became a lot less polite and much colder. "This is a lot of money, Max. Millions that I have smart people diversifying and investing well for you. I'm thinking an annual payout might be the best way to make sure it isn't wasted."

Max met his brother's infamously cold green gaze with eyes just as cool, if not more so. "You said if I got married you'd sign the paperwork. Were you lying?"

"No, I wasn't," Cole answered. "But contrary to what you seem bent on believing, I'm not your enemy, Max. You're my brother, and I want what's in your best interest."

"You mean you want to control me, just like Granddad wanted to control me," Max spat back.

Cole was the golden boy and Max was the screwup. Their grandfather had handpicked Cole and groomed him from a young age to take over the Benton Group when he died. Max, he'd just tried to manage.

Manage him as Cole was trying to do now that it was time to hand Max the reins to the money their grandfather had put in trust for him. Cole had gotten his payout at the age of twenty-five, no questions asked. On Max's twenty-fifth birthday, he'd found out through their lawyers that his grandfather had increased the payout age on his trust to thirty-five without bothering to tell him.

His grandfather had carried little faith in Max back then, and Cole seemed to hold even less faith in him now.

"I'm not trying to control you," Cole said, his face terse. "Maybe if you told me why you wanted all the money in one fell swoop…"

"Because it's mine," Max answered, cutting him off. "I wasn't aware I needed your approval to spend *my* money."

Cole looked at him for a hot, angry second. Then his green eyes flicked over to Pru. "Pru? Do you know what Max is planning to use the money for?"

Max glared, only now seeing the trap Cole had laid out

for them. He'd known Max wouldn't tell him. So he'd put the question to Pru. If Pru didn't know the reason, if he was keeping secrets from her, then that would give him enough leverage to declare their conveniently timed marriage an obvious fake and refuse to sign over Max's trust.

He began to open his mouth to say that what Pru did or didn't know wasn't any of Cole's damn business—since it wasn't. But Pru stopped him, squeezing her hand over his.

"Yeah, I do know," Pru said, and that was all she said. She didn't give Cole any more information than what was needed to satisfy his question.

"And do you approve of these supposed plans of his?" he asked.

Pru surprised him by answering without any hesitation at all. "Actually, I do approve, and I think you should sign over the money."

Cole seemed jolted by her answer. He looked at her hard. So hard Max knew he was searching for any sign that she was lying to him. Any sign at all that he could use against his brother.

But Pru met his gaze without flinching, her brown gaze level and unfailing.

"Fine," Cole finally said, sounding none too happy. "I talked to the family lawyers, and they say they're going to put a rush on getting the trust paperwork together. It will probably be ready by your birthday on Friday."

Today was Sunday, which raised a question. "If the papers aren't ready yet, why did call us up here?" Max inclined his head toward Pru. "We could have gone somewhere and enjoyed a honeymoon while we waited."

Cole also inclined his head, but to the opposite side. "Yes, you could do that. Still could if you want. Or if you're interested, Pru, I have another case for you."

Pru blinked in surprise. "Me?" she asked. "But I still don't have my license yet."

"No, but you, unlike the other licensed PIs I hired, actually found my brother. And now that you've married him, you're in the unique position to help me with a problem we're having at the Benton Group."

Pru sat forward, the expression on her face both flattered and curious. "Tell me about it."

"Well, as you know, over the course of the fall, we're planning a multicity launch for the Benton Inns, a midrange brand of hotels that will cater to our customers who used to have a lot of disposable income but have now settled down with families and are more interested in saving money than spending it in our casino resorts. Our first open will be in New Orleans. But over the last few months, the launch has hit a few snags."

Cole got up, as if this next part of the story agitated him too much to tell it sitting down. "Key Card Hotels, our largest future competitor, has somehow figured the specifics of what this first hotel needs to open its doors and has been consistently sabotaging our efforts. Outbidding us for important contracts, planting news stories with a negative spin on certain planned aspects of our first project—things like that. Many of these acts of sabotage are so specific that it's become obvious to me Key Card must have an inside source at the Benton Group."

Pru nodded, leaning even farther forward as Cole filled her in on the details of his case. However, Max eyed his brother, more than a little suspicious. First he'd invited them up here, knowing full well the trust papers weren't ready to be signed, and now conveniently enough, he had "a case" for Pru.

"I don't get it," he said after Cole was through. "That sounds like corporate espionage. Don't companies call in security firms to handle stuff like that?"

Cole nodded at him once, seemingly impressed that Max had even that much knowledge of how corporations actually worked. "Yes, usually that's exactly what I would do.

Call in a security firm to root out the saboteur. In fact, I still might do that. But first I want to try a different approach."

He turned back to Pru. "When I told Sunny about your solving of the case, she said she wasn't surprised. She said you had a one hundred percent track record for the cases you took on for the other showgirls, because you're good at the research aspect of the job, but also because you have good gut instincts. That's how you found Max, right?"

Pru shot a quick glance at Max, probably wondering quite rightly if this current line of conversation at all insulted him.

Max just squeezed her knee and threw her one of the looks of love she'd taught him. "I've never been so happy to be found," he said to his brother, while still looking down at her.

He liked the way she blinked back at him, her hand, perhaps unconsciously, going tighter on top of his. And her voice sounded a little strained when she said, "Guts and research. It's not the most sophisticated method, I know."

Cole nodded. "Well, I think you might have what it takes to solve this case, too. As you may or may not know, this is a retreat for the Benton Group's entire senior management team, nationwide. Everyone's coming in today, and I'm pretty sure one of these top-level executives is the one responsible for leaking info to Key Card. I want you to talk to them, see if you get any gut feelings about who it might be. Of course, I'll pay whatever fee you ask and a per diem."

"You want me to stay here all week?" Pru repeated. She shook her head. "But how would we explain that to your team? I'm a retired showgirl, and isn't this retreat supposed to be execs only?"

Cole answered with a small smile. "That's where Max comes in."

Chapter 9

By Monday morning, Max was beyond miserable. Not only had Wedding Night Pru not made a much-fantasized-about return, but she'd also spent hours in Cole's room putting together a dossier on the group of executives who would be joining them at the retreat on Sunday. The first presentation meeting was scheduled bright and early at 9:00 a.m. on Monday.

Max knew this, because in order to give Pru a good alibi for being in Utah on this retreat, he'd be required to make like the prodigal son and attend the meeting. According to the cover story Cole had concocted for him, Max had seen the error of his ways, and now that he was married, he was being welcomed back to the Benton Group with open arms. Luckily the title of "brand ambassador" had always been open for interpretation, so claiming that Max suddenly wanted to be involved in the Benton Group at the executive level shouldn't be too hard to pull off.

The whole situation set Max's jaw on edge, but it wasn't as if he could refuse to play the part. Even he knew that any real husband wouldn't allow his wife to turn down a job she wanted because he didn't feel like going to a week's worth of meetings.

However, Max Benton was not a meetings kind of guy, and he didn't know what stuck in his craw more: that Cole had gotten him exactly where he'd been wanting him ever since he started nagging Max to join the Benton Group in a real capacity, or that Cole had dragged Pru into the screwed-up mess that was their brotherly relationship.

With PI Pru spending most of Sunday evening in his brother's room, Max was left with nothing to do but sketch out more plans for his first hotel. He must have fallen asleep while waiting for Pru to get back, because when he woke up, his pad and pencils were all collected on the room's wooden desk. There was a piece of hotel stationery lying on top of the pad with a note written in efficient cursive.

"Borrowed your car to drive home and get some more clothes. Back tomorrow afternoon. I like this one."

Max looked to the pad and saw it had been turned to the third possibility he'd sketched for his New Orleans hotel's nightclub. His first sketch had imagined the club with a heavenly theme. The second with a devil's playground effect, and the third was a mixture of the both. Pure Good meets Unapologetic Bad.

He'd liked this vision the best himself and was glad Pru agreed. Maybe after they signed the paperwork, she'd agree to come back with him to New Orleans for a little bit. She could study for her licensing exam there while he put the details in order to start building on the hotel.

Max stopped that thought dead in its tracks. Look at him, acting as if he and Pru were a real couple. He just wanted to finish what he'd started with her, he reminded himself. Get the promised night of passion out of the way and then go their separate ways after he got his money.

Max liked a challenge, and Pru was proving to be a bigger one than most. But at the end of the day, he knew himself. He'd be bored with Pru as soon as he she was caught.

He just had to catch her.

A knock on the door interrupted his thoughts about his lovely prey.

He answered it to find Cole already dressed in a suit. One that was a near match for the one he held out to Max on a hanger.

"Figured you might need something appropriate for the

meeting," he said. "And you're about the same height as me. See you downstairs."

Max grimaced at the suit. "Who wears a suit on an executive retreat?" he asked.

"You do," Cole answered with a smirk.

He thrust the suit at Max and walked away before he could protest any further. Cole was right about the fit of the suit, however. Though it'd been tailored for Cole, it fit Max fine. However, that didn't make it comfortable. He much preferred the kind of suits he wore to nightclubs, light trendy ones that didn't reek of office work.

Thirty minutes later, Max found himself around a long table in the lodge's conference room with a bunch of guys and about five women, all wearing suits similar to his. There was maybe one guy other than Cole and himself under the age of forty, a Latino dude who had taken a seat on the other side of Cole. The guy looked as if he used even more product than Max to keep his hair slicked down in a classic clean cut straight out of a Ralph Lauren ad.

Cole introduced Max to the group with the cover story he'd concocted about his younger brother having finally decided to take an interest in the Benton Group and his role as brand ambassador, now that he was newly settled down. It was word for word the vision Cole would have had Max adhere to if he ruled the world, and Max had to put major effort into not rolling his eyes as Cole spun his fantasy. After that, the group went around and introduced themselves to him and each other.

It was the usual suspects. A bunch of senior managers from the various casino-resort properties, and quite a few executives from the main Las Vegas office, many of whom Max had met before at the annual board meeting. The Latino guy turned out not to be as boring as the rest of the executives around the table. Cole took the lead on his introduction, inviting the gathered group to congratulate their newest VP, Gustavo Martinez. Apparently he was some kind of hotel wunderkind who'd been recruited straight out of Cornell and had worked his way up to senior management at the Benton New Orleans before he'd even hit his late twenties.

Now at the tender age of thirty-one, he had been trained by Harrison Connors—the soon-to-retire vice president whose job he was actually taking over—and Cole himself. Cole's involvement was what caught Max's attention back from the short list of designers he'd like to work with on his own hotel.

From what Max had seen, Cole never took an interest in the younger execs. In his brother's mind, you either did your job well or you got cut from his team—no mentoring required. But either some of Sunny's natural altruism had rubbed off on Cole, or he'd taken a genuine interest in this guy, because he was grooming him for an even bigger role in their company than vice president.

Given his recent dealings with Cole, Max doubted it was the former. And his suspicions were confirmed when instead of conducting the first presentation on the Benton Las Vegas himself, he handed the floor over to Gustavo.

First he thanked Cole for "that great introduction." He had a very Southern flavor to his accent, Max noticed. Louisiana through and through, even if he was dressed up in a suit at an executive retreat in Utah.

"I'm not that fancy. You all can just call me Gus," Gustavo said to the rest of the table. Then he launched into a speech about what he and the rest of the management team had planned for the Benton Las Vegas, the original Benton property, over the next few years. If Cole had a stockier build, a slightly Cajun accent and a lot more charm, he'd be Gus, Max thought as he listened to the guy deliver his long presentation. No wonder his older brother was so into this guy.

But even Gus couldn't make a presentation filled with number projections all that interesting. Max was about ready to mentally check out on the rest of the speech, when Gus said, "And here's something our newly reinstated brand ambassador will find interesting…"

He went on to say that the Benton Las Vegas was currently in negotiations with Grey Soul, a popular Top 40 DJ, for a residence year at the Max.

"Why?" The one word slipped out of Max's mouth before he had time to remember that Cole had forced him into this meeting and that he wasn't really interested in any of this.

Gus looked down at him, his charming smile still on full beam. "Why?" he repeated, as if Max's question were completely incomprehensible. "Because he's one of the biggest DJs in the world right now."

"Yeah, yeah, yeah," Max said. "And he just came off a resident year at The Abelli. One of the Benton LV's biggest competitors."

Gus's smile stayed put but came down a few watts. "Yes, we'd be stealing him away from The Abelli, which is why this would be a great coup."

"You're thinking like Cole now," Max said, interrupting him once again.

Another quizzical look from Gus. "And thinking like the man who's led the Benton Group into unprecedented profits is a bad thing because…?"

"Because Cole thinks about everything as a battle between us and our competitors—which is a good thing when you're talking about business. But what you're doing—what you're supposed to be doing with the Max nightclub isn't about business. It's about psychology, about compelling the right people and controlling how our customers view the Benton LV."

"I know that. That's basic marketing," Gus answered. "And we've got one of the best marketing companies in LA primed and ready to design a new campaign for the Max when we get this DJ."

"That's great, Gus. Good work," Max said. "I'm glad you and the rest of management are ready to spend a ton of money telling our patrons that we've now got The Abelli's leftovers, because that's how it's going to look to them. Not like we stole him, but like we now have yesterday's news. Because they're not going to know or care about whatever you went through to secure this guy. All they're going to see is sloppy leftovers."

Silence filled the room. But Max's point must have hit home because the impressed look had fallen off of Cole's face, and a few of the other execs seemed to be mulling over what Max had said.

Also, Gus was no longer smiling. "And what would you suggest would be a way to put Max in the spotlight?"

"Less Tack. More Lux. All Gamble," Max answered.

Their grandfather's original six-word mission statement for the Benton brought Cole's head around to Max. "Keep talking," he said.

So Max did. "Granddad didn't want the Benton doing what every other hotel was doing in Vegas. That was his thing from the start. He took a risk building a sleek and modern hotel back in the age of glitz, and if we want to do this Granddad's way, we don't go after the latest thing. We take a gamble and go after the *next* thing. That's how you get the clientele you want. You get the DJs that only rich guys who have the money to party in Ibiza know about."

Max had no idea he had so much to say on this subject until fifteen minutes passed and he'd given Gus not only a list of DJs to pursue for monthlong resident spots, but the celebrities who wouldn't have to be paid to make an appearance at one of their gigs.

And it didn't stop there. Later on during Gus's presentation, he also discovered he had a lot of opinions about their plan to hire the same design firm that'd done the last set of updates back toward the beginning of the millennium. And a few suggestions for East Asian cities they'd left off their list to run Benton Las Vegas ad campaigns. Gus's presentation ended up going well over its allotted two hours, and by the time Max made his last point, it was time to break for lunch.

As all the execs were standing to leave, Cole said to the room, "I suggest you all take notes about what went wrong during Gus's presentation. Use the time before your presentation wisely. Reconnect with your teams and make sure your presentations won't fall apart if Max asks you the same marketing questions he has asked Gus."

No one was more surprised by this announcement than Max. He'd thought this was all supposed to be an act. But judging from the way a few of the executives rushed out of there, they were actually planning to rework their presentations in order to garner Max's approval. Also, Gus, who remained behind, didn't look nearly as confident as he had at the start of the meeting.

He approached Cole with downcast eyes. "May I have a word with you, Mr. Benton?"

Cole leveled a displeased look on Gus. "Later," he answered. "I have a few things to go over with my brother."

Gus's jaw tightened, but he gave Cole a quick nod and followed the rest of the executives out. Soon Max and Cole were the only two people left in the room.

"Must be hard for the guy," Max observed. "Actually giving a damn about what you think."

Cole didn't answer, just smirked at Max.

"What?" Max asked, though he already knew.

Cole just continued to stand there, smirking.

Max shook his head. "I was bored," he told Cole. "I figured why not mess with your carefully crafted Cole clone. What else did I have to do?"

Cole gave him an appraising look. "Yes, that must be it. Either that or you have a lot more of Granddad in you than he ever gave you credit for. More than I ever gave you credit for."

Max wanted to roundly deny Cole's assessment. He was nothing like their grandfather, who'd been even stodgier than Cole. As far as Max could tell, he'd ever done only two exciting things in his life: married their grandmother, Nora, who had been a showgirl when they met, and founded his own hotel.

But then Max thought about his plans for the New Orleans property he was developing and closed his mouth.

Mistaking his silence for agreement, Cole stood up and said, "You're going to fit into the Benton Group just fine. Let's go have some lunch. You can tell me all about the reconnaissance work you were apparently doing on the Benton's behalf by partying all over the world."

Cole's words were actually dangerously close to the truth. Max had decided to start his own hotel using little more than his past experiences with hotels and nightclubs of all types to develop his own property. But Cole didn't know that.

"Pru should be getting back anytime now, and I promised I'd take her into town for lunch," Max lied.

Of course Cole invited himself along.

They went back and forth for a few minutes, before Max gave up and decided to just have lunch with his brother in the common room with the rest of the executives. He doubted Pru would appreciate having to play the part of his wife at a restaurant with Cole anyway.

"I'll just stay here and have lunch with you," he said to Cole.

Cole didn't even try to hide his smile over winning their latest battle. "Probably for the best," he said, guiding his brother out of the conference room. "We wouldn't want to arrive late for the rest of the presentations. The CEO not being there on time reflects badly on the whole company."

Max was about to tell Cole where he could put the rest of his sure-to-be-boring presentations, when he stopped short, his eyes narrowing.

Gus Martinez stood at the bottom of the lodge's main staircase, with one hand wrapped around a suitcase Max recognized from New Orleans, partly because its owner was close by. Pru, dressed in a green polo top and hot pants, smiled up at Gus as they talked near the stairs.

Max clenched his back teeth. Apparently his wife had returned from Vegas, and Gus had taken it upon himself to welcome her back to the Sinclair Lodge.

Chapter 10

There was a very handsome man standing outside the Sinclair Lodge doors when Pru pulled up in Max's yellow Ferrari. He had a gloomy look on his face and what looked like a lollipop lodged into the side of his mouth.

She immediately recognized him as Gustavo Martinez, Cole's new VP hire, but of course, she wasn't supposed to know that. So when she got out of the car, she just gave him a friendly wave before heading toward the back of the Ferrari to retrieve her bag.

He, however, seemed to have no such qualms about revealing that he already knew who she was. "Prudence Washington," he called around the lollipop as he jogged over.

Then he lifted her bag out of the trunk before she could and said, "How's it going?"

Despite the lollipop, he was outrageously good-looking, she noted with the distant assessment of an investigator doing her job. He also had a very charming Southern accent. So down-home, it made her feel as if they already knew each other.

"I'm great…um…" She trailed off, so that he'd supply his name and she wouldn't have to keep on pretending she didn't know it.

"Gustavo Martinez, but everybody calls me Gus." He shifted her suitcase to his left hand, so that he could extend his right one for a shake.

"Former smoker?" she asked him as they made their way toward the lodge's front doors.

"How did you know?" he asked, his head tilting with surprise.

She pointed to his lollipop. "A few of the girls on the line used lollipops to tide them over until their next cigarette."

Gus removed the lollipop and chucked it in the trash can to the right of the doors. "Well, I've quit for good. Mostly I just use them for when I want to smoke but can't."

Pru grimaced with empathy. "First meeting that bad?"

He answered with a wry laugh. "And long. It was also my first time presenting—I started at the Benton right after you retired."

"But you know who I am," Pru said.

"You're kind of famous, since you're still in all the hotel's print campaigns for the Benton Revue. There are even a few with Sunny floating around, and she's been off the line for nearly two years."

"Well, we haven't exactly been replaced yet," Pru observed. She kept her words circumspect, but she had a feeling that Gus, being one of the few Latinos in upper management, would understand her meaning.

Sunny and Pru had been the only two black dancers on the line. Now that they were both gone, there were exactly zero black women dancing on it. But like most hotels that attracted a diverse clientele, the Benton wasn't exactly out to advertise that it didn't currently have any African-American dancers on its revue line. So Sunny and Pru had remained in many of the print-ad campaigns.

"No you haven't, but I'm sure Sunny's gonna make sure that's no longer an issue when she takes over as lead choreographer in the fall. *Then* we'll shoot some new ad campaigns." He winked at her. "That's a promise, Miss Washington—though I guess I should call you Mrs. Benton now, right? Saw that crazy wedding video of yours online yesterday."

Pru stumbled to catch up. "Yes, I suppose you could call me Mrs. Benton," she answered, though she had no intention of taking Max's name, considering they'd be filing for divorce by the following Monday. "Or you could just call me Pru like everybody else."

"Okay, if you want me to call you Pru, that's what I'm gonna call you." He threw her a smile that probably had slayed many a woman's heart in Louisiana, and held the lodge door open for her.

Inside there were several other executives she recognized from the short dossiers she'd compiled on them with Cole's help the night before. The smell of hot food lingered in the air, and the majority of them were either standing in line or loading up their plates, which meant they must have just broken for lunch.

She scanned the common room and didn't see Max in line or at any of the long tables that had been set up for dining. Nor did she see Cole. Maybe they'd decided to go out for lunch.

"I see you went and got yourself a haircut, Pru," Gus said, falling back in step beside her as they headed for the stairs.

Pru raised her hands to her now extension-free locks. She'd gotten them taken out this morning and was now sporting a short kinky-coiled pixie cut. The shorter length already felt like a great relief after years of wearing long extensions, and she quickly found she didn't miss having long hair at all.

She patted her new do and said, "Yeah, I thought it was time for a change."

"Change looks good on you," he told her as they headed over to the stairs together. "Very good. Makes me wonder how Max Benton got so lucky."

Pru waved off the compliment. "I'm sure most people who saw that wedding video are wondering how I got so lucky."

Gus stopped at the bottom of the stairs.

"Well, I'm not most people, Pru, and I like to call things

like I see them." His eyes twinkled as he looked down at
her. "In this case, I'd say, Max is definitely the lucky one."

"Yes, I am," Max said, suddenly appearing at her side.
He slipped what felt to Pru like one very possessive arm
around her shoulders, and then used the other one to pull
her around so that she was now facing him instead of Gus.

"You're back," he said to her. And that was all the
warning she got before he laid a kiss on her. One so bone
melting that she momentarily forgot about Gus, or any of
the other businesspeople currently occupying the lodge's
nearby common area.

The kiss might have gone on forever, if Max hadn't
eventually lifted his head and murmured, "I missed you."

"I missed you, too," she said softly, the words tumbling
out of her mouth without conscious thought.

A slow and ridiculously smug smile spread across his
face as he said, "Good."

Then he took her bag from a wide-eyed Gus and all but
hauled Pru up the stairs and back to their room.

"What was that?" Pru demanded as soon as they were
back in the room.

"Me saving you from a guy with crap taste in DJs," Max
answered, closing the door behind them. As soon as it shut,
he reinserted himself into her personal space, getting way
closer than he needed to, to say, "You're welcome."

Pru took a step back. "I didn't need saving."

Max took a step forward. "I think you did. This morning I found out that Gus is the kind of guy who likes stealing what isn't his. For the good of the plan—you know *the
original job* you're getting paid for—you'll want to stay
away from him."

Then in what felt to Pru like a total non sequitur, he said,
"So I'm pretty sure Wedding Night Pru put in a cameo during that kiss. Can you let her out again? Because we have
some unfinished business."

He leaned down, and Pru had to put her hands on his chest to stop him from advancing. "There's only *me* here. And for the good of the *case* I'm also working on in order to maintain our original story, if Gustavo Martinez is the kind of guy you say he is, I probably don't want to stay away from him. In fact, since he seems to enjoy flirting with me, I should probably use that as an in to get closer to him."

An angry scowl flashed across Max's face. "Closer how?" he asked, pressing against her hands as he moved in even closer.

She could feel him now, against her stomach, his arousal long and hard and obvious. Pru swallowed. Apparently she'd accidentally hit Max's competition button.

Even more reason she should make solving this case her number-one priority, she decided. The sooner she did, the sooner she could reasonably get out of here and back to her life in Vegas, far away from her fake husband.

Once again feeling flustered by the Benton heir no one was supposed to take seriously, she retreated several steps back, only to run into a wall.

Max closed in, placing a hand on each side of her head.

"Let me assure you, Detective Pru," he said, running his nose along her neck, "whatever you want from Gus, I can give you. Let Wedding Night Pru come out to play and I'll give her whatever she needs."

It was just the tip of his nose touching her now, no other part of his body, but the small action sent a shiver of sexual tension through her entire frame.

"His wallet," she somehow managed to rush out. "What I really need is Gus's wallet, so that I can access his personal information. And his phone, too. So if you really want to give me what I need, help me get them."

Max paused and she could see the muscles in his shoulders bunch as if he had to hold himself back from just taking what he wanted. But eventually he pulled away, his face tight with what she could only guess was frustration.

Max, she knew, wasn't a man used to not getting exactly what he wanted, exactly when he wanted it.

But all of a sudden, he frowned and said, "You got rid of your extensions."

Pru looked from side to side, her face scrunching up with confusion over the sudden topic change. Also because she wasn't used to men directly referencing her weave.

"Yeah," she answered carefully. "I got rid of them."

A hard look came over his face then. One so harsh, it made her wonder how he'd ever managed to garner a reputation as a happy-go-lucky guy in the first place. "You got rid of them, because you were trying to get rid of her. Trying to make yourself under, so I'd be less attracted to you."

Well, she wouldn't have called it a "makeunder" per se. She loved the way she looked with short hair and thought the tight little pixie fro would really complement her mostly vintage wardrobe. But other than that…yeah, that was exactly why she'd made sure to toss her extensions before coming back to the Sinclair Lodge.

"I've got work to do here, and all that extra hair was getting in the way."

This time it was Max who took a step back, the look on his face so lethal, he put her more in mind of a hit man than a brand ambassador for luxurious sports and leisure.

"One hour," he said, his voice low.

"What do you mean 'one hour'?" Pru asked, once again flummoxed by the sudden change of subject.

"You want Gus's wallet and phone. I want an hour with Pru. Not Detective Pru. Wedding Night Pru."

Pru shook her head. "Are you saying you want me to get drunk again?"

"No, I don't want you to get drunk. I want you to get real." Max crooked his head to the side. "In my experience, and I have a lot of it, people either become someone totally different when they're drunk or they show their true colors."

"And you think it's the second one when it comes to me?"

"Sweetheart…" The hot up-and-down look Max gave her made Pru feel as if she was slowly being stripped bare. "I know it is."

Then before she could argue with him any further, he turned and left the room. Leaving Pru to wonder if he'd really get Gus's wallet and bring it back, or if Max was just toying with her.

Pru was pissing Max off. First of all, hot pants? Seriously? He wouldn't have minded the modern-day version favored by adult movie stars and strippers alike. He'd seen so many of those throughout the years, they seemed ubiquitous now, and he barely noticed when women wore them anymore.

But the high-waisted orange ones Pru had chosen to wear today ought to be against the law. The sophisticated cut and the low back hem made them tasteful enough to wear outside a nightclub. Nonetheless, the hem was still high enough to show off her long, shapely legs to perfection. And though they didn't mold her skin like spandex, they framed her assets enough for any red-blooded man to know there was something juicy underneath. Know and want to take a bite.

Judging from that kiss they had shared at the bottom of the stairs and the sexual tension that had been thrumming between them when they argued earlier, she wanted to take a bite of him, too. They were two adults. Why not enjoy their time stuck in Utah together?

Yet she resisted him at every turn. Acted as if he'd made up the fun, passionate woman he'd met on their wedding night. Well, he was done playing that game—at least the one she wanted to play with him. Red-hot fury flowed through him as he pulled out his phone and charged down the steps. He pressed his brother's name and typed in two words to the text box. Play along.

A few hours later, Max charged back into the room to find Pru at the desk, reading something on her laptop.

As he got closer he could see it was an article. One with a picture of a younger Gus standing in a suit with his arm resting against a banister in the familiar pose of a student so overachieving, the school just has to write a feature article about him. It was the kind of article no one would bother to read unless they were digging deep into a person's life.

Research and guts. Max thought back to their earlier conversation with Cole, and knew for sure that Pru had just spent the past few hours researching another man the way she'd researched him before tracking him down in New Orleans.

Jealousy ran through his bloodstream like an unstoppable river. Max felt hot with anger and also like an idiot, because he understood that this was what Cole had basically asked her to do.

It also didn't help when Pru not only did not look up from her computer when he came into the room, but also asked, "Hey, did you know your grandfather handpicked Gus out of Cornell's hotel administration program to start out as a manager at the Benton's New Orleans location?"

Max hadn't known, but he wasn't surprised. Cole had graduated from the program before moving on to another Ivy League school to get his MBA, and his family had long been charitable supporters of Cornell's esteemed hotel administration program.

But Max hadn't come up here to talk about Gus. "Pru, turn around."

Pru's shoulders stiffened, and she very carefully kept scrolling down the screen. "I need to finish reading this article, and then I have a few more leads I want to investigate—"

Max reached around her and very deliberately closed the laptop on Gus's overachieving college face.

Ignoring Pru's gasp of indignation, he repeated, "Turn around."

She did, probably only because she wanted to give him a piece of her mind. Which made it even more satisfying for Max when she froze in shock, her mouth dropping completely open at the sight of what he was holding in his hands.

A basket with not just Gus's wallet and smartphone but also the wallets and smartphones of all twenty-two of the other executives attending the retreat.

"So," said Max, not even bothering to keep the note of triumph out of his voice, "when do I get Wedding Night Pru back?"

Chapter 11

It took quite a few attempts before Pru was able to form words, much less complete a sentence. "What…how… there's no way." She swallowed and finally got out, "How did you do all of this?"

Max smirked, enjoying her shock immensely. "Let's just say when it comes to suits, never underestimate the power of a trust exercise. You've got these for about thirty-six hours until our breakfast meeting on Wednesday, then I have to give them all back."

Pru's entire face lit up. "Oh my gosh, I can't believe it. This is exactly what I needed. Thank you so much!" she exclaimed, reaching for the basket.

Max had to admit it was nice to be on the receiving end of her gratitude as opposed to her complete disdain for once on this trip. But still, end goals were end goals.

He lifted the basket away before her fingers could make contact with it. "Uh-uh-unh, Prudence. Nothing comes for free between us. You of all people should know that."

Pru's eyes widened. "This is your brother's case, involving your family's company," she reminded him. "You should want to help me solve it."

"Yes, I should," Max agreed with a lazy shrug. "But I've always been a selfish bastard, so I'm just going to continue on that route and withhold this basket of juicy intel until I get what I want."

Pru's eyes narrowed now. "You wouldn't."

Max answered with an incredulous look. "I'm paying you to be my wife in order to get my brother to sign off on my trust fund," he answered. "Not going to lie, Pru, I'm kinda shocked you keep putting stuff past me."

He then lifted one of the smartphones out of the basket. "Did you know that shockingly few of the people on our executive committee have passcodes on their phones? They've left them wide-open, primed for info gathering."

With an irritated sound, Pru made a sudden leap to snatch the basket away from him.

A leap that Max, who'd played lacrosse from an early age all the way through college, easily sidestepped. He raised the basket above his head with one hand and placed the other against her forehead, admiring the view of the way her chest heaved under her terry-cloth polo as she wildly attempted to get at the basket. Eventually she gave up with an angry squawk of frustration.

"This isn't fun and games, Max!" she reminded him, full-on Detective Pru. "This is about the future of your family's company. And if I only have thirty-six hours with them—"

"So yeah, it's probably in your best interest to agree to my terms sooner than later," Max finished for her.

He set the basket on a side table and leaned against its edge, putting his entire body between its contents and her.

Perhaps sensing that he would more than enjoy having to intercept her if she made another attempt to get at the basket, Pru folded her arms and lifted her chin. "Fine. You can have an hour with me in exchange for the basket. But I'm telling you now, I'm not opening my legs for you."

Her words made a dark wave of lust pulsate through his body. He was going to enjoy proving her wrong on that count.

"An hour with Wedding Night Pru," he coolly reminded her. "And an hour will only get you Gus's wallet."

"But how about the rest of the wallets?"

"Same deal. An hour for each wallet."

This announcement sent Pru into full sputter. "But—

but that's impossible. There has to be at least twenty wallets in there."

"Twenty-two if you count Cole's and mine, which you don't need. So yes, I guess we can call it twenty, and I can be a generous man when I want to, so I'll throw in the matching phones, too. Free of charge."

From the look on Pru's face, she didn't consider his offer as generous as he did. "You want twenty hours with me for the basket, and I only have thirty-six hours to go through them?"

"Twenty hours with Wedding Night Pru," he corrected. "And let's say you give me one hour up front. I could take the rest after the thirty-six hours are up."

Pru's eyes once again narrowed. "First of all, let's just say there is a Wedding Night Pru. There's no guarantee you're going to get what you want from her. And even if you do, what's to keep me from reneging on my nineteen credit hours after I get what I need from the basket?"

Max half smiled, almost liking how unwilling she was to go down without a fight. "Nothing," he answered. "Except the fact that you don't lie."

Pru shook her head at Max, not understanding his reasoning at all. She was totally a liar. She'd lied to him from the moment they'd met again in New Orleans, and she was lying to his brother about the real nature of her involvement with him now.

As if reading her mind, he said, "You see, right around the time we were having that first convo with my brother, it occurred to me that I've never actually heard you lie. Even your story about why you were in New Orleans was perfectly crafted to let me assume you were there with a bachelorette party and not specifically for me. I bet you even had a flight out at the time you said you did."

Pru's cheeks warmed. Actually, he was right. Her flight

details had been the absolute truth and she'd gone straight to the airport after leaving his hotel room.

He took her silence as an invitation to keep going. "And with Cole, you were careful never to reference love when it came to me. I also don't think you were lying to him about what you thought of my plans for the trust money."

That was true, too. Pru looked away to hide the fact that he'd totally found her Achilles' heel.

"But you know what really let me know you've got a thing about not lying?" he asked. "The fact that you've never out-and-out denied the existence of Wedding Night Pru. You know she's in there, and you're holding her hostage for some reason—maybe for the same reason you don't lie."

Again, that totally exposed feeling came over her. As if Max had stripped her completely bare without one touch of his hands.

He nodded, as if she'd affirmed with her silence every single thing he'd said. "So yes, Pru, I'll take that gamble. If you say you'll let me have twenty hours with the Pru I met on our wedding night, I believe you'll let me have her."

He pushed away from the table and closed the space between them in an instant. "So how about it, sweetheart? Twenty hours with Wedding Night Pru. Are you willing to take that gamble with me?"

"Twenty hours," Pru repeated, weighing the words. "But I can't drink," she told him. "Not when I'm on a case."

"Like I said before, I don't want you drunk," he replied. "I want you alert and sober for every single thing I plan to do to you."

His words sent a shiver down Pru's back. "And—and how about if I solve this case? L-like tomorrow? If that happens I should be able to go back to Las Vegas and you can go back to wherever until you have to sign the papers."

Max gave her hypothetical a few moments of consideration before shrugging and saying, "Fine, Pru. If you solve the case, any remaining wallet hours will be forgotten."

Pru rubbed her suddenly sweaty palms on the front of her hot pants, trying to make a decision she didn't want to make.

It was only an hour, she told herself. And the old Pru wasn't a complete idiot. She partied too much, and made quite a few piss-poor decisions when it came to men. But even on her most outrageous night, it had taken more than an hour to seduce her.

So if she let the old Pru take over for an hour, that didn't mean she'd be having sex with Max. Max wasn't that good. And the old Pru wasn't that bad…she hoped.

"Okay, fine," she said. "One hour up front and the rest later." *Hopefully never*, she added silently. Then she asked Max, "Do you want the first hour after dinner?"

It's business, she told herself. *Just a deal you're making to solve this case, which will lead to other cases and make it so you never have to deal with men like Max Benton ever again.*

"No," Max answered, his eyes hot on her. "I want my hour now. I want her back now."

That was fine. She could give him the old Pru for an hour right now, and maybe he'd even get so frustrated when she turned down his advances that he wouldn't bother with the other nineteen.

She told herself this as she went over to the desk, picked up her phone and set a timer for sixty minutes before propping it up sideways against her closed laptop.

Then she made herself meet Max's eyes just as the old Pru would have looked any man directly in the eye. Especially one as fine as Max. "Your hour starts now, Max."

She issued these bold words and braced herself for another one of his fiery kisses, but it never came.

Max just stared at her while the clock on her phone finished counting down the first full minute. Then he said,

"Welcome back, Pru. Let's celebrate your return with one of my favorite games, Truth or Dare." He gave her a feral smile and steepled his hands like a villain personified. "I'll start. Truth or dare, Prudence?"

Pru wet her lips, more than a little scared now. She'd been playing Truth or Dare since high school, and the old Pru had one hard-and-fast rule for the game. She always chose dare.

"Dare," she told Max with a tight chest.

Max's vicious smile grew even wider. "I'm guessing your underwear is vintage, too, Prudence. Let's find out."

Pru hesitated, realized the old Pru wouldn't have and then pulled her terry-cloth polo off quickly to reveal the bandeau rainbow bikini top she was wearing underneath. She'd spent the morning washing clothes, and like many women around the world, had put off the task so long, she'd been forced to wear a bikini as she did so.

"Hot pants, too," he said.

She stepped out of them, thinking the joke was on him as she revealed the bikini's full-waisted electric-blue bottoms.

It's literally a bikini, she reminded herself, and a rather modest one at that. No big deal. Like standing in front of Max in her swimsuit. She couldn't even tell if he liked what he was seeing, since his gaze remained just as it had before. Completely amused and totally wicked. As if he was having the time of his life laughing silently at her.

Annoyance rippled through her. "Do I get a turn or is this a one-sided game of Truth or Dare?"

One black eyebrow lifted and he answered, "Sure, sweetheart. I'll take truth."

"Great, tell me the truth," she said, her newly bold eyes meeting his. "This is just a game for you, isn't it? I turned you down, and your ego couldn't take it, so now the only reason you want to go to bed with me is so you can have me and trash me, just like all the other girls. That's why they call you the Ruiner, right?"

His eyes grew a few shades cooler. Then he said, "You've got me, Pru. I do want to take you to bed. I want to spend this week figuring out what turns you on and then I want to use what I discover to make you scream and make you come harder than you ever have with any other guy. And then, yes, after I'm done with you, I will walk away."

He stepped closer, and Pru found herself instinctively steeling, refusing to back down this time. She didn't flinch, not even when he leaned forward to say in her ear, "But before I do that, I will ruin you for any man who comes after me."

His tone was soft, but his words were so vicious, it felt as if they were ripping through Pru, cutting her dignity into pieces.

Max let a few seconds tick by before asking once again, "Truth or dare?"

"Dare," she answered immediately, welcoming the change of subject from Max's "plans" for her. Now wishing she hadn't asked about them in the first place.

"You should have picked truth," he said. "Sure you don't want to change your mind?"

He still hadn't touched her, but the sexual tension was back. Buzzing between them like an electric magnet.

Pru's legs began to feel a little weak, but she shook her head in answer to his question. The old Pru wouldn't have backed down.

There came a moment of silence so suspended, it made Pru feel as if she was at the top of a roller coaster. Then he said, "Dance with me."

He reached into the basket and pulled out his phone. A few seconds later a fairly new club anthem that Pru recognized from the night of their nightclub wedding played. The song sounded thin and weak coming out of his phone, stripped of its previously overwhelming power to make her want to move her body.

But after eight years on the line, she knew how to dance

when it was the last thing she felt like doing. She swayed her hips, giving Max a sexy show. At the same time, she glanced at the countdown timer. A little over forty-five minutes to go.

Only now did Max touch her, grabbing her by the wrist and saying, "I said, dance *with* me."

She'd heard him. But didn't understand what he wanted from her.

He answered her unspoken question, tugging on her wrist and draping it over his shoulder before pulling her in close and tucking his face into her shoulder.

And suddenly the music didn't sound so weak anymore. In fact, it came through loud and clear, pulsing through them as they swayed to its rhythm as if their bodies were one. Pru's eyes drifted closed, letting the song work its magic. When it finished, another one took its place and then another one after that.

Eventually, she forgot where she was and whom she was with. Max became another part of her, swaying when she swayed, his hips moving with hers.

It made it hard to know whose idea it really was when she turned in his arms, dancing with her back to his front. More memories from their wedding night came rushing back. How she'd tossed her headdress into the crowd so that they could dance just like this. How his breath had felt on the back of her neck. Thrilling and hot.

"You're starting to remember," he said behind her.

She was.

"Nod," he said. His hand was on her belly now, and she could feel him hard and thick against her back. "Let me know you remember."

She nodded, knowing it wasn't a great confession. She'd always remembered the dancing part of that evening.

"What else do you remember?" he asked.

"That's all," she answered. "Just the dancing."

"So you don't remember what happened when we got back to the hotel room?"

Pru froze, going stiff in his arms. But it didn't matter. He kept them moving, making both of their bodies sway to the music as he asked, "Are you locking up because you remember or because you don't?"

"I don't remember," she told him, not to be mean or to bring him down a peg, but because it was the truth.

"Then let me give you a recap. We danced like this and then I got us a room, so that you could sleep it off—you see, Pru, occasionally I can be a gentleman. But in this particular case you made being a gentleman very hard for me, because as I was tucking you in, you were begging me to do you. Your words. Not mine. 'Just do me, Max,' you said. 'Let's keep the party going.'"

His words echoed in her ear, causing her entire body to heat with something she might have been able to attribute to embarrassment, if its origin point hadn't been between her legs.

"You grabbed my hand and forced me to touch you here."

His hand found her breast, rolling her nipple through the bikini's top and causing her to gasp. But Max continued on, his voice casual and low. "And you begged me to take you, Pru."

He continued to torture her nipple, rolling it through the fabric, causing liquid heat to pool between her legs. Then he cupped her roughly with his hand, squeezing the lips of her mound together through the blue bikini bottom.

Pru's back melted into his chest and somewhere in the distance a woman moaned. Was it her? She didn't know. Couldn't tell. There were too many sensations going on in her body now, making her mind fuzzy, making her pant.

Once you go Max, you never go back.

"Truth or dare?" she somehow managed to squeeze out. A pause. Then Max's voice was back in her ear. "Truth."

"How many other women have you played this game

with?" she demanded. "How many other women have you decided to ruin?"

She needed something. Needed something that would convince even the old Pru that giving in to Max wasn't a remotely good idea.

But his answer came harsh and unexpected. "Only you," he said. "I've never set out to intentionally ruin any woman but you, because no one else has ever pissed me off as badly as you do."

He punctuated this statement by moving his hand up from her mound. But this turned out to be only a momentary reprieve. Soon it was back on her belly, slipping inside her high-waisted bikini, down, down until Max found what he was looking for. And pushed two fingers inside it, brushing her clitoris with the ball of his hand as he did so.

On purpose? She had no idea. Her body bucked all the same, her throat releasing a loud involuntary moan.

Two fingers began pumping into her with slow, knowing strokes. "Was this what Wedding Night Pru wanted when she begged me to touch her?"

It was. She was sure of it, but he hadn't said "truth or dare," so she didn't have to answer that, she reminded herself, as her head fell into her chest, her whole body slumping because of what he was doing to her.

But Max kept her on her feet. "Don't worry, Pru, I've got you. Just give me another one of those pretty moans to let me know you're still with me."

She did moan. Moaned hard, but she couldn't be sure if her answer was voluntary, because it felt as if Max's fingers were pulling the broken sound out of her.

Her moan seemed to be the answer he needed, because he went to work after that, pressing the ball of his palm into her clit. This added an overwhelming pressure to his hand action that felt both delicious and cruel. In a way that made her want to beg him to stop and implore him to keep going.

Not that it mattered. At that point she couldn't have formed words if she tried. She was too busy biting back a scream.

The orgasm, when it came a few minutes later, took her in one greedy swallow, sending her into a vortex of pleasure before it spit her back out, weak as a bowl of jelly.

Now it really was Max holding her up. Keeping her tight against his chest as his fingers continued to pump into her afterglow.

"Pru, Pru, Pru," he crooned in her ear. "You are very wet now. And extremely tight. How long has it been?"

Again, she didn't answer. Didn't have to, she reminded herself as her head lolled from side to side. She didn't have to do anything now but close her eyes and let the old Pru take over. Let the old Pru get everything she'd apparently begged for from Max.

But suddenly he stopped, pulling his fingers out of her. "Truth or dare?" he said quietly.

Pru blinked, confused and frustrated. Despite the orgasm he'd given her, she was still throbbing down below. Because of him. Because of what he'd done to her. And she no longer wanted to play this game.

"Why? Why do we have to do it this way? Can't you just take what you want?" she asked him. Only after the words were out of her mouth did she realize that he didn't have to answer her questions either. She hadn't said "truth or dare." Also, it wasn't her turn.

"Truth or dare?" he said again. This time the three words were hot and hard in her ear.

"Truth," she spit out, both her past and present selves agreeing that they didn't have the guts to take another dare from Max Benton at this juncture. And maybe he would ask a different question this time.

But he didn't.

"How long has it been?" The question was an angry demand.

One she didn't understand. Why was he asking her this? Why did he care?

"Truth," he repeated when she didn't immediately answer. "How long has it been?"

"A long time," she whispered.

"What do you qualify as a long time?" he asked.

Anger mixed in with the lust, confusing her, making it so she didn't know what to do. Was he accusing her of being a slut, after all the women he'd run through? Trying to make her prove she was worthy of him or something? She had no idea.

She averted her eyes, even though he was standing behind her and couldn't see her face as she answered. "Like, over five years. Is that long enough to prove whatever you're looking to prove?" she asked.

However, letting him know that she'd actually been as prudish as her name suggested for over half a decade didn't seem to make Max happy.

His entire body stiffened, and he cursed. Once, twice, then a third time as he brought his forehead to rest against the top of her head. "Listen, sweetheart," he told her, his voice ragged, "you're very wet. But I need you even wetter, because…"

He broke off with another curse, and he finally let her out of the clinch. Turning her around to face him, before dipping his head so that they were at eye level. The wicked gleam was gone now, replaced by a brutal honesty that sent a frisson of fear through her belly.

"I'm not going to be able to hold back with you," he told her. "I'm going to take you, and it's going to be rough. So I need you to lie back on the bed and let me make you come at least once more, so I can make sure you're ready for me. I don't want to hurt you. Let me take you with my mouth first. Please."

Pru's heart was beating fast now. Too fast. So fast, it didn't seem healthy.

Run! a small voice whispered inside her. *Don't let him.*
She tensed up, preparing to bolt. But then…she didn't.

And that was when Pru knew that the old version of
herself had fully taken charge. Because instead of running
screaming from the room, Pru pulled away from Max…
and climbed into his bed.

The old Pru didn't care how fast her heart was beating. She wanted this. She wanted Max. And it was the old
Pru who lifted her eyes to Max. Waiting to see what he
would do next.

Chapter 12

"You were thinking about running, weren't you?" Max asked, meeting her gaze head-on.

Apparently he wasn't the type to back down either.

Pru didn't lie. "Yeah, I was."

He started stripping out of his clothes, ditching the suit jacket and white dress shirt, pushing the pants down and kicking off the shoes. All without dropping her gaze.

"But you didn't," he said, coming to stand at the edge of the bed, in nothing but a pair of boxer briefs. All traces of playful Max were gone now, as well as the slightly desperate man who'd pleaded with her to let him get her off with his mouth.

This switch did not make the old Pru change her mind. And her eyes wandered down his body to the only piece of clothing left on it. Not to be titillating but because she couldn't help but look at what was encased there, straining to get out.

"No, I didn't," she answered, her voice little more than a murmur.

Max followed her gaze and gave her a thin smile. "Maybe you should have."

Before the threat could fully sink in, he had her by the ankles, pulling on them so hard, Pru fell backward, legs flying in the air. Making it easy for him to reach forward and jerk the bikini bottom off her hips and down her legs in one savage yank.

Then he was on his knees between her legs, shoving

them wide as his tongue dived deep inside her, his nose pressing into her clit.

Pru bucked, even worse than she had when he'd touched her there. His mouth felt exactly like an invasion, and he didn't let up, just pressed her back down onto the bed. Then his fingers got in on the action, parting her lips, opening her even wider for his complete and total takeover.

He owned her with his mouth, devouring her and tormenting her with his fingers until she fell apart. Her hips lifted in the air as a second climax ripped through her.

"Exactly what you wanted," came his voice, gruff and smug. Then he was above her, his long and lean body stretching toward the nightstand.

He had his boxer briefs down and the condom dealt with before she'd even finished coming down from her high.

Then he was between her legs, long and thick. Pushing in.

Pru's breath caught.

And Max cursed. "So tight," he said, his voice strained to the point that she couldn't tell if this was a compliment or a complaint.

But then he answered her question, capturing her eyes again and shaking his head at her as if she was the naughtiest girl he'd ever met. "I'm trying not to lose it with you, but you're making it hard for me, Pru."

He began moving inside her, his strokes measured, giving her time to adjust to his size as he went in, deeper and deeper. "But you like making things hard for me, don't you, sweetheart?"

His strokes became harder, sharper, filling her up in a way that felt like a punishment delivered inside a Trojan horse of pleasure. "You liked making me wait for this like a dog, hoping to get his treat. But now I've got you. Exactly where I want you. Exactly where you've wanted me to be, since the first time we kissed in New Orleans."

Max was everywhere now, heavy body on top of her,

heavy erection inside of her, heavy voice in her ear, making nasty accusations. The scent of their combined arousal filled up her nose, acrid and obscene, not allowing her to deny his words or anything else that was currently happening.

Yes, she wanted this. What woman in her right mind wouldn't?

But Max wasn't satisfied with her nonanswer. "Talk to me," he growled. "Let me know how much you want this. How good this feels for you. Give me a reason to hold back."

He pushed into her so hard on the last sentence, the stroke hit her clit, causing her to cry out at the unexpected extra pang of sharp pleasure.

"I do want this," she gasped helplessly, clawing at his shoulders as the pleasure of that last stroke vibrated through her.

Then she showed him. Really showed him the real Pru. "But I don't want you to hold back."

Max stopped pumping. Both his nose and his eyes flared with shock.

Pru felt like a live wire, her entire body pulsing with a dangerous sexual current. She met his gaze. Met it as the old Pru would have and said it again. "I want you. I don't want you to hold back."

Max became an animal on top of her then. Wild and crazed, riding her so hard the line between reward and punishment became impossibly thin.

When the orgasm came, it blasted all the way through her. A nuclear bomb, taking out everything in its path. Her voice, her vision, her hearing. Every single breath of air in her lungs.

And when she came down, what felt like years later, she could hear the sound of her phone's timer chirping in the background. And Max muttering something in her ear.

If not for the fact that he was now collapsed on top of

her and no longer moving, she would have had no idea that he'd come, too.

"What...?" she croaked, feeling like a bomb victim. "What did you say?"

Her voice seemed to bring him back from whatever edge he'd been on.

He abruptly stopped muttering. Pulled out and raised up off her, getting out of bed. A few moments later, her phone stopped chirping.

She tried to follow his movements, but her eyes wouldn't cooperate. Her whole body felt sluggish, like something that had been put through a wringer.

Still, her curiosity held on, made her ask again, "What did you say?" even as her eyes fluttered close.

"Nothing," came Max's answer from far away in the room. Clipped and hard. "I didn't say anything, Pru. Go to sleep."

She followed his command, not necessarily because she wanted to, but because sleep already had her in its clingy grip.

Chapter 13

*N*ot enough.

Those were the two words that had appeared inside his head last night after he completely lost it with Pru. The words that kept on repeating inside his head when his orgasm hit him like an electric shock wave. Causing him to lock up and lose all sense of time and place until he finally came down, mumbling the words out loud.

Not enough, not enough, not enough...

What the hell did that even mean? He'd gotten what he wanted from Pru. It should have been enough. More than enough. He should already be bored by now, coming up with plans to put some distance between him and Pru, so that sharing a room for the next few days wouldn't become awkward.

Instead the words had been stuck on a loop in his head for the past thirty-two hours. Making it hard for him to think of anything more than Pru. The taste of her sweet essence, the sound of her sweet moans, the feel of her sweet body receiving him, allowing him to go as hard as he liked. Telling him that was what she wanted.

He had ended up putting at least some distance between him and Pru. Leaving their room early and coming back super late, just so he could leave her alone for the thirty-six hours she had with the wallets and phones he'd procured for her.

He would be giving the wallets and phones back to the other execs at their breakfast meeting today. Then he'd have to wait until lunch for another hour with Pru.

It was 5:00 a.m. now, which meant seven more hours until he could have her again. Max seriously wasn't sure he could wait that long. If anything, the two words seemed even louder now inside his head.

Not enough, not enough, not enough...

"Max, did you hear anything I just said?"

Max looked back over his shoulder at Cole, who was holding up the other end of the canoe they were carrying toward the water.

"Nope," he admitted. "But I'm guessing it was something boring about business."

"Something boring about canoes, actually. I was just asking how much you weigh, because usually you want the heavier person in the front. I think that's me, but in this case, I should probably be in the back. That's the best place to guide."

"I know how to row, Cole. Just because I wasn't on the rowing team at our boarding school like you doesn't mean I can't handle myself in a canoe."

"Maybe not, but it does mean that you don't understand the value of working as a team, or taking guidance for the greater good. This is supposed to be a team-building exercise, remember?"

Max did remember. That was just one of the reasons he considered this entire canoeing excursion not worth even a minute of his time. Along with the fact that he'd had to get up at the butt crack of dawn in order to participate in this useless exercise. But it was either this or a morning spent in the room with Pru, watching her work on the case, when all he wanted to do was cash in another wallet before her thirty-six hours were up.

Not enough...

And though Pru had worn a relatively demure khaki dress the day before, Max had spent all day embroiled in fantasies about unfastening each button and devouring whatever he found underneath.

So he signed up for the stupid canoe trip. Him, along with nearly every other executive at the retreat. They were either eager to suck up to Cole or needed a way to handle the smartphone withdrawal Max and Cole were putting them through, supposedly in order to become closer as a team.

However, when Cole had arrived at the boathouse where all of the lodge's canoes were stored, instead of choosing one of his sycophant executives to share his canoe, he'd chosen Max.

And now here was Cole, already trying to boss him around before they were even in the water. They were only a couple of years apart in age, but Cole continued to act as if Max was the little brother he used to be. The damaged kid who'd arrived at boarding school needing his big brother to take him under his wing.

Things only got worse when they were out on the water, with Cole playing commander in the back of the canoe, telling him which side to paddle on. As if he was a child, without instinct or sense.

"Look, I'm not into the whole taking-orders thing," Max told his brother when they were a few good yards in front of the rest of the Benton executives. "So if you need that to make this team-building torture exercise of yours enjoyable, then we should probably paddle back to the rest of the group, so that you can switch out row buddies. Where's Gus? I'm sure he'd love to have you at his back, telling him what to do with his paddle."

Cole, as usual, chose to ignore Max's not so thinly veiled insults. "Gus is back at the lodge," he answered, his voice chilly. "Harrison can't come because of his sprained ankle, and Gus asked if they could use the time to put together another stab at their Benton Las Vegas presentation. That's what I like about Gus. He's not lazy. In fact, he always goes the extra mile to show his commitment to the Benton Group."

"Yeah, yeah, yeah, he does a better job of being a Benton than your actual brother does. That's why you love him. You and Granddad, both," Max answered.

Behind him the sound of Cole's steady rowing came to a sudden stop. "What do mean about Granddad loving Gus?" he asked.

Max looked at him over his shoulder. "Granddad hand-picked him for the Benton New Orleans. You didn't know that?"

Cole shook his head. "Is this something Pru dug up?"

"Yeah, that, and his hardscrabble backstory. Born with a congenital heart defect. Abandoned by his mom at the hospital. Dad raises him only to up and die when he's three, so the New Orleans foster-care system basically raises him. But his congenital heart defect pretty much makes him unadoptable. But eventually he gets a new heart, and he goes on to win one of the Benton Foundation scholarships to attend Cornell, even though he's never stayed in a hotel himself. Seriously, you didn't know any of this? Granddad didn't tell you anything about this guy?"

A frown came over Cole's face. "No, Granddad never mentioned him. The only part I knew was that he'd gone to Cornell on a Benton scholarship. But a large number of our management recruits can make that claim."

Now it was Max's turn to frown. Hearing Gus's sad backstory had actually curbed a little of the animosity Max felt toward the guy. Even after he'd spent nearly all of last night's dinner hour in the common room flirting with Pru. But the fact that Cole had no idea about any of Gus's background raised several red flags.

"Weird. Most of the execs I've met would have made sure everyone knew if they had a backstory like that. They would have put it in their corporate bio."

Cole agreed with a nod, adding, "All Gus's bio says is that he grew up in Louisiana, went to Cornell and was general manager of the Benton New Orleans by the time he was thirty. That's impressive, but even more so, given his background. Maybe he's ashamed of it?"

"Maybe…" Max said, his head tilting as he brought the paddle back down to take another swipe at the water.

"But you don't think so," his brother said, reading his mind.

Max thought about the way Gus had finagled himself into the seat on the other side of Pru during dinner the night before. He had used just about every weapon in his charm arsenal to keep her attention off Max and on him. They'd laughed over mutual friends at the Benton Las Vegas and the fact that spending most of their adult lives working for a Benton had ensured that they would never ever gamble.

Gus had not only managed to drop his vice president title several times, but had also alluded to what he would do for the Benton Revue now that he had it. He'd told Pru so much about himself that Max had found himself having to tangle with another bout of dark jealousy. Gus had obviously been trying to make it known to Pru and anyone else within earshot how much he had in common with her. And how much Max, who'd pretty much spent most of his adult life hotel hopping in the hottest party cities in the world, didn't.

Yet, Gus hadn't mentioned any of the personal details Pru had dug up on him.

"I'm just saying he doesn't seem like the kind of guy who doesn't know how to properly toot his own horn. And not mentioning that Granddad recruited him—that's kind of shady."

The fact that Cole didn't jump to his golden boy's defense meant that he thought so, too. He picked up the paddle and said, "The next time you see Pru, tell her good work and to keep digging on Gus."

Max nodded, though he already knew that next time he saw Pru, they wouldn't be talking.

Chapter 14

Max wasn't there when Pru woke up on Wednesday morning. She wasn't surprised this time. At first she'd pegged Max to be the kind of guy who stayed in bed until after lunchtime and filled his days with leisure and partying. But so far he'd proved the opposite. Not only had Max attended all the meetings for the retreat but when she'd woke up the morning before, she'd found him typing something into a laptop. A tool she hadn't even been aware he possessed, much less brought on the trip.

"What are you doing?" she'd asked him.

He'd immediately closed the laptop and swiveled to face her, claiming it was nothing.

Pru didn't think it was nothing. But she already had a case she was working on, so she'd let it go.

However, this morning he wasn't even in the room when she woke up, and the sight of the empty bed caused a small twinge to go off in her heart. One she didn't care to examine, since what she had with Max was technically a job. A job that Max had chosen to overcomplicate with his stupid sex demands, but a job, nonetheless. The best thing she could do right now, she thought, was forget what happened on Monday night and work on solving the case as quickly as possible. Then she'd have a good excuse to leave Utah before Max could redeem too many more of his wallet hours.

With her plan made, she moved to get out of bed, only to be served up another reminder of Monday night. Her sex was still tender nearly a day and a half later. It released a dull ache as she sat up, making it impossible for Pru to forget how his lips had felt against her core, the way his tongue had worked in perfect synchronization with his fingers inside her. Or about the rough way he'd taken her, his battering strokes so good, she wouldn't have stopped him, even if she could have predicted the soreness it would cause her later.

As she gingerly climbed out of bed, she remembered his response to her question about whether they'd done it on their wedding night.

If we had hooked up last night, you'd have no doubt about what had happened, because you would be feeling it this morning. All over your body.

She had to admit he'd been right… A cold shower. The thought dropped down like a lifeline in an otherwise stormy ocean. That would be her first order of business and then she'd get back to work.

But when she said *cold*, she didn't mean ice-cold, which is what the shower in their en suite bathroom produced.

"Sorry about that," the lodge manager said when she called down to the front desk. "Those upstairs bathrooms are on a separate water heater from the rest of the lodge. I'll call maintenance in. Meanwhile you can use the common showers downstairs if you don't want to wait."

She didn't want to wait. Five years of mothering her brother had taught her to take care of personal hygiene first thing every morning. That, or risk the day and any chance of a shower completely slipping away from you.

Plus, she wasn't at all squeamish about the common-shower situation. She'd shared a dressing room with over forty other women and at least a dozen male dancers for most of her working life. Common showers were nothing compared with that.

But before she went downstairs, she called over to Harrison's room. Last night at dinner, she'd volunteered the use of their en suite bathroom to the older executive, after finding out that he'd been forced to go all the way down to the common bathroom on the first floor in a boot, because of the ankle he'd sprained shortly before coming to Utah.

Her research into Harrison had revealed the nearly retired exec to be a sterling employee who had served the Benton Group as a vice president for over twenty years. And, he was an even more first-rate citizen. Not only did he tithe to his church, but he had also given generously to several Las Vegas charities, including Nora Benton's lung-cancer nonprofit.

Making the offer hadn't felt like a hardship, but the exact right thing to do, given what Pru knew about him. But now she was calling him to renege on the offer, which made her feel almost as guilty as fake marrying Max for money.

However, it wasn't Harrison who answered his room's phone, but Gus.

"Oh, did I call the wrong room?" Pru asked, looking at the phone's digital readout display. "I'm looking for Harrison."

"And you found him. Nearly everybody else is on that team-building canoe trip, but I stayed behind with Harrison to work on a presentation. I came up to his room, because—"

"Because he sprained his ankle," Pru finished for him.

She then quickly relayed the information about their out-of-service bathroom for Gus to pass along.

"Sure, I can tell him that," Gus said. "Anything else I can do for you, Pru?"

The way he leaned on her name conveyed all sorts of innuendo, and Pru shook her head. Apparently the wedding ring that she wore whenever she left the room mattered nil to Gus.

"No, that's it," she answered, deciding against asking him if he had a robe she could borrow for her trip downstairs to the common showers. Gus totally struck her as someone who would take that kind of question as a double entendre.

Besides, like Gus said, nearly everyone, including her temporary husband, was on the canoe trip anyway. She jogged down the stairs and into the common showers as fast as she could, reminding herself that a towel covered up a lot more than an itty-bitty rhinestone bikini.

The shower was just the thing she needed. Not only did it take her mind off Max, but it also gave her some time to think about her next move.

She'd have to return all the wallets and phones today, which meant she would no longer have the benefit of tracking the execs' communications without being detected.

Also, her most promising lead was turning out to be a bit of a bust. Despite her strong initial gut feeling that Gus wasn't quite what he seemed, she couldn't find any evidence that he was the mole giving away corporate secrets.

As far as she could see, he didn't intimately know anyone in high positions at Key Card. Partly because he'd always worked for the Benton New Orleans, and partly because he was so much farther ahead in his career than his peers. Key Card was actually based in Arizona—not Louisiana. And no one in Gus's graduating class three years before or after outranked him. Even his classmates who'd found jobs at Key Card weren't in important enough positions to coordinate this kind of information steal.

Added to those facts, Gus's record was totally clean. No arrests. No large debts, and he'd finish paying off the few college loans he had the year before. The only large purchase he'd made had been very recently—a Corvette convertible, bought the day after he officially moved to Las Vegas. Again, not a red flag. Buying a car after receiving a huge promotion was pretty much an American rite of passage as far as she knew.

However, that meant she was no further along in her case than she'd been before she received the wallets. No closer to solving it, and no closer to getting away from Max.

But that would change today, she decided, turning off

the shower and pulling her towel down to dry herself off. She'd managed to secretly sign all of the phones up for a tracking service that would let her know when and where all the devices were at any given time. She'd also concocted a plan for Cole to drop a key piece of information at to-night's not-yet-announced camping trip. Material so tan-talizing their mole would definitely want to pass it on to Key Card as soon as possible. Between being able to track the phones and the fake-info plant, she should be able to bring this case to a close by midday Thursday.

Feeling optimistic after her shower and plan review, Pru wrapped the towel back around her body and stepped out of the stall with a new spring in her step.

Only to run straight smack into Gus.

She stumbled backward with a gasp, but luckily Gus, who evidently hadn't even been swayed by their collision, caught her by the arm.

"Whoa, Pru, you okay?" he asked, flashing that easy-going smile of his.

"Yeah, I'm fine," she answered, quickly taking her arm back.

Apparently Gus hadn't been as worried about covering up with a robe as she had been. He was also dressed in nothing but a towel. Probably because, with all his thick muscles, he looked like the after picture her brother had been pursuing all summer.

And he seemed to enjoy flaunting it. While she used her hands to make sure her towel was firmly in place, he put his hands on his hips, giving her a full view of his broad chest and accompanying six-pack of abs.

However, Pru was way more curious about the long thin scar running down the center of his chest. It was only barely noticeable on its rock-hard tableau, but the evidence that he'd had heart surgery still drew her eye. Until she re-alized that Gus probably thought she was checking out his impressive body.

"Sorry, I didn't think anyone else was in here," she said, quickly raising her eyes to his face. "I should have been watching where I was going."

Unlike her, he didn't bother to hide that he was checking her out. "I should have been watching, too. But I can't truly say I'm sorry I bumped into you," he answered. "I've been up all morning, working on this new presentation with Harrison, and I've got to confess, looking at you is a nice break from looking at him."

"Um…thank you, I guess," she said, feeling more than a little bit uncomfortable.

She respected Gus a lot for what he'd been through and the obstacles he'd surmounted. But this was the third time he'd unapologetically flirted with her despite knowing that she was a married woman. Even in her wildest years, she'd carried a basic respect for marriage vows. One that Gus didn't seem to share.

As if reading her mind, he gave her another up-and-down look. "Like I said before, Max is a very lucky man, landing a wife like you. Beautiful, savvy, willing to settle."

She inclined her head, feeling weirdly defensive of Max, despite the supposed compliment on Gus's part. "I doubt any other woman would think I settled."

"That's because they only notice Max's appearance. A lot of women don't mind dating a man without any ambition, but you seem smarter than that to me. More like your friend Sunny. Someone who can easily move in and out of Las Vegas circles. Someone who'd be comfortable at a charity ball or a nightclub opening. Not every woman has what it takes to serve her man well as a Vegas wife. And women who do—women like you—shouldn't settle on just any man."

Pru kept her face carefully blank, trying to figure out if he was serious or if this was some kind of deep corporate spy game he was playing with her. "Well, thank you for letting me know your thoughts on my recent marriage," she said after a few disbelieving moments. "I'll keep them in mind."

"You do that," he said with another killer smile. "And if anything changes after this Friday, look me up when you get back to Vegas. I know someone on his way up who would be very interested in a girl like you."

This time Pru couldn't keep the shock off her face. Friday was Max's birthday. The day he'd officially receive his trust money—the day he'd officially be free to divorce her.

Gus knew about Max's inheritance. Knew and must have guessed that what she and Max had was more of a monetary agreement than a true marriage.

She narrowed her eyes, prepared to press him further on the subject. But before she could, a voice said, "What are you doing in here with my wife?"

Chapter 15

Max had never been a jealous man. In his life. In fact, the few women he had officially dated for longer than a few nights had been the type who went out of their way to turn heads. And it had never bothered him that other guys coveted what he currently had.

But walking in on Gus and Pru, both dressed in nothing but towels, bothered him. His lips curled into a sneer as he directed his attention toward Gus. "What are you doing in here *with my wife*?"

Gus turned to him with a condescending smirk on his face, muscles flexing as he lowered his hands to his side.

"I just came down here to take a shower before this morning's round of presentations," Gus answered, his voice a near drawl. "Imagine my surprise when I found such a beautiful sight. Must have been serendipity."

The towel and the new set of clothes Max had brought to change into quickly ended up on the shower room's floor as Max started toward Gus.

But Pru stepped in front of him. "Max," she said, "you dropped your clothes on the floor. Do you want to go back to the room with me? Get some more?"

"No, I don't," Max answered between clenched teeth. "I'd much rather stay here and punch this guy out for daring to look at another man's woman."

Gus tilted his head. "Really? Because that's how I heard your parents met. Wasn't your dad still with Cole's mom when he got her sister, your mom, pregnant? Or is that just hotel gossip?"

Max pushed forward. Only Pru's hands pressed against his chest kept him from going farther.

"Max, please don't…" she said, her voice desperate. Though she hadn't looked all that surprised when Gus had dropped that nugget of scandalous Benton family lore. Yet another thing she must have found out before hunting him down in New Orleans.

Feeling like a fool, Max decided to back down. But not politely.

"Don't worry, sweetheart, I won't hurt your sad little admirer," he said to Pru, throwing Gus a cold smile. "Looks like you've had some major heart surgery there, desperado, and I'm a charitable man from a charitable family. I'd never forgive myself if I did anything to make you need more surgery, which of course we Bentons would have to pay for, just like we pay your salary."

Pru's eyes widened. "Max!" she gasped.

But he didn't care. It was true, he wasn't about to go after a guy who'd had heart surgery. But he also for damn sure wasn't going to just let him get away with flirting with Pru.

Gus took a step toward Max. "That surgery was a long time ago, man, and I assure you, I can more than take care of myself if you want to do this."

"He doesn't," Pru answered for Max. "And more important, I don't want you to, because there's nothing to fight over. Max, we were just talking, I swear. And Gus, if you're going to take a shower, go take it, please. More people are probably going to be getting back from the trip soon, including my brother-in-law."

Gus looked between her and Max as he clenched and unclenched his fists. But perhaps sensing that it might not be the wisest thing for his career to get into a physical fight with the younger Benton, he backed down.

"Never let it be said that Gus Martinez would turn down a beautiful woman's request. Sure, I'll go take my shower now," he said, his eyes outright challenging Max. "See you later, Pru."

Pru didn't answer, which was a good thing. Max couldn't have been responsible for his actions if she had in any way responded to the heavy flirtation in Gus's voice.

Pru stood there, her hands still on Max's chest as they both watched Gus disappear into one of the shower stalls. A moment later the water came on, and Pru let out a breath of relief.

A breath was all she got, because in the next moment, Max had her lifted up in his arms, carrying her to the closest hidden space.

"What are you doing?" she demanded in a whisper when he set her down and shut the door behind them. The bathroom's metal locking device slipped closed with a jingling clang.

The front of her towel was nearly undone now, hanging on to its tuck by just a tip. A tip Max reached out and undid with just a flick of his finger.

His nose flared when the towel fell away, and his member came to thick life inside the jeans he'd worn on the canoe trip. It was angry and ready to be inside her.

"Cashing in a wallet," he answered.

He cupped her newly uncovered sex then, needing to feel her, needing to know if she was slick with her own arousal. Her sex pulsed in hot invitation.

It was an invitation he took, pushing three fingers into her and biting down a groan when her tunnel clenched around his fingers with hot need.

Her head fell forward onto his shoulder, her whole body melting into his touch, even as Detective Pru protested, "You said I had thirty-six hours."

"You need to revisit the language of our agreement. I said I could give you thirty-six hours," he murmured against the top of her head. "*Could.* I never guaranteed I would."

She whispered a word, one that wasn't very kind, but she didn't push him away. Just whimpered and gripped his shoulders, helplessly watching him guide her hips as he made her ride his hand.

Damn if she wasn't just about the sexiest sight he'd ever seen. So sexy that his own painful need became background noise as he watched her naked body pumping into his hand. Her whimpering became louder and louder until eventually her mews turned into full-on moans and her hips started moving faster against his hand.

Max's own arousal became untenable then, and though he hadn't meant to take it this far, he stopped.

"What…why did you stop?" Pru looked adorably dazed and confused, which made Max move even faster with the condom he'd brought out of his pocket. He didn't want to leave her feeling abandoned any longer than he had to.

In mere seconds he was fully sheathed, his jeans around his ankles.

"Pru, sweetheart, I know you don't want anyone to hear us, but—" he lifted up one of her long legs and wrapped it around his waist at the same time that he began the long push into her wet tunnel "—I'm going to need you to get loud for me. Think you can do that?"

He pushed the rest of the way in, and Pru gasped, her eyes widening with pleasure. But then she shook her head. Shook her head even though Max could feel her core tightening around his shaft, already milking him with her need.

She was fighting it. Fighting him, and that made Max pick her up, pressing her hard into the stall's wall as he wrapped her other leg around his waist, too.

"Are you trying to make me mad, Prudence?" he asked, pushing into her with short, jerking strokes that rubbed her clit both on the way up and on the way down.

Her body caved into his, obviously overwhelmed by the sensations Max was producing inside her. But she remained mutinously silent, clamping her lips together and shaking her head. Refusing to do his bidding. Refusing him.

Max's strokes became vicious. He barely held on to a thin edge of self-control as he took his wife. Marked his claim. "I need you to understand something, sweetheart," he whispered viciously in her ear. "While you're here, you belong to me. No one else."

Pru answered this time, her voice little more than a broken gasp. "Y-you need to revisit…th-the language of our agreement. I was—I was speaking to Gus, for the case… case is my first priority—not your st-stupid pissing contest with G-Gus."

Her breathless words burned through Max, and that wild feeling came over him again. The one that made him feel as if he couldn't get close enough to her even though he was all the way inside her.

"Unless you want me cashing in my wallets at very inconvenient times, I suggest you make *me* your first priority," he growled, thrusting into her even more savagely.

Then, before she could even think to respond, he brought his hand down and pinched her most sensitive place, brutally triggering her orgasm.

She did scream then, but soundlessly. Her head falling back as her hand circled around his wrist, trying to push it away.

"Too much," she seemed to be saying, and he could feel the intensity of her climax, her core nearly locking him in.

But he didn't stop. He continued to drive into her, continued to torture her clit, so that she couldn't escape the orgasm, couldn't escape the pleasure's unrelenting assault.

And she soon lost her battle to stay quiet, helplessly screaming out. So loud that there was no way Gus couldn't hear her, even with the noise of the shower.

What Max didn't expect was to join her. Instead of reveling in the satisfaction of her surrender, the entire lower half of his body involuntarily pushed him into Pru's tight space as deep as he could go, releasing into the condom as if compelled by her helpless screams.

He yelled out then, just as loud as Pru, and then he went completely mute. For moments on end, he couldn't talk, couldn't breathe, still couldn't get close enough to Pru as he finished releasing into the condom.

Not enough...

He was in trouble. He knew now that what had just happened between him and Pru wasn't his usual fun and games, but something much more. Because he hadn't broken their implicit agreement and taken her in the bathroom stall just because he could.

No, the real reason he'd taken her like this was because he wanted her to know that for the time being, she was his. His alone. Not Gus's.

This was crazy. This needed to stop. This needed to stop right now.

Not enough...

What the hell was he going to do? he wondered as the orgasm finally subsided. How was he going to get this girl out of his system by Friday? Breathing hard, he looked down at Pru and saw his own fear reflected in her brown eyes.

A tap suddenly sounded on the stall's door.

Pru's eyes went wide, and she began shaking her head frantically.

Her unspoken request brought a much-needed dose of amusement back into the situation for Max, and he arched his eyebrows at Pru. That cat was most definitely out of the bag, thanks to her screaming.

"Yes, Gus?" he answered, unable to keep the self-satisfied note of triumph out of his voice.

"It's not Gus, it's Cole," came his brother's dry voice on the other side of the door.

Now Pru was really mortified. She shook her head and covered her eyes with both hands.

Max just answered, "Yes, Cole?"

"A reminder that the other execs weren't allowed to bring significant others on this trip," Cole said. He somehow sounded both annoyed and amused. "Let's not give them any reason to be jealous."

Max had to work hard to keep the chuckle out of his own voice as Pru uncovered her eyes and shoved at him. Perhaps she hadn't realized that both her legs were still wrapped around his waist, and that he was the only thing keeping her pinned to the wall.

"Will do, bro," he answered, clamping one of his hands around one of her wrists to keep her from battering him. "Thanks for the heads-up."

"You're welcome, Max." Cole waited a beat before saying, "And good morning, Pru. Sunny told me to tell you she's looking forward to seeing you on Friday when she gets here."

Pru cringed for several seconds, seemingly stuck in a paralysis of complete embarrassment.

But eventually she managed to squeeze out. "Good morning, Cole. I'm looking forward to seeing Sunny, too."

"Perhaps the four of us can go out for lunch that day. Celebrate Max and me signing his papers."

"Sounds great," Pru answered, her voice laced with discomfort.

"Good, good, I'll have my assistant make reservations," Cole said. He then finally walked away, leaving a very embarrassed Pru and a rather amused Max in his wake.

Chapter 16

Perhaps not surprisingly, things got awkward between Max and Pru after what happened in the downstairs showers.

But not at first. At first Pru had been the only one caught up in embarrassment. She didn't slip out of his grip until she heard the sound of Cole's shower being turned on. As soon as that happened, she climbed off Max, rewrapped her towel around her body and dashed out of the stall. She then shot up the stairs to their room as fast as her bare feet could carry her.

Max reappeared in the room about twenty minutes later. She could feel his eyes on her back, watching as she pretended to be so wrapped up in her case notes that she didn't notice him come in. But to her relief, he didn't call her bluff, just headed for the closet.

She listened to the sound of him changing and somehow resisted the urge to peek over her shoulder at him while he did so.

She sat tight for about fifteen excruciating minutes, then came the sound of the room's door opening and closing. And he was gone again without either of them having said a word to each other.

She spent their time apart trying to figure out a way to show her face at breakfast the next day when she could barely work up the nerve to text back and forth with Cole about tonight's plan. For once she wished she hadn't left the old Pru so far behind.

She probably would have just laughed.

But then again, who really knew what she would have done, because it wasn't as if the old Pru had ever had the kind of sex she'd had with Max. Tits, butt, legs and sass— she used to think those were her best assets, and her relationships had been a reflection of that. Back then she'd worked at being a good trophy girlfriend. And when it came to what happened in the bedroom, it had been more about her putting on a good show than actually being pleased by her partner.

Until Max.

Pru had never ever experienced anything like what she'd had with Max. Twice. And that scared her, the memories of what he'd brought out in her, making it hard for her to concentrate on her work, even after he'd left the room.

Luckily for her, the Benton execs spent all morning in meetings. Then, according to the lodge's manager, instead of getting lunch catered as usual, they'd all gone to Kanab, a town about thirty miles away, to eat.

Pru was happy to grab a sandwich out of the lodge's vending machine and use the extra time to make sure everything was in place for tonight. By the time Max returned to the room, carrying quite a few shopping bags, she had a pretty good grip on her emotions.

"Looks like you did some shopping," she said.

Not the coolest observation ever, but at least she was able to keep her voice casual. Maybe it wasn't completely obvious that her insides were still quivering with the memory of how thoroughly he'd possessed her body that morning.

Max didn't answer, just deposited the bags on the bed.

She tried again. "How did giving back the wallets and phones go? I tried to cover my tracks to make sure no one knew I'd been rooting around in there, but you can never be sure."

No answer, and Max pulled a new backpack out of one of the bags, a sleek and hardy nylon number that looked as if it could easily withstand both wind and rain.

"Going somewhere?" she asked, as if she didn't already know.

This question finally got a response. "Escalante for a surprise camping trip," he said, through what sounded like gritted teeth. "Cole just announced it. We're leaving in twenty minutes."

Her eyes widened with pretend shock. "Whoa, short notice."

She wasn't surprised Max was in such a bad mood. He didn't seem like the type of guy who belonged anywhere near a campground.

Feeling a bit sorry for him, she went over to the bed and picked through his bags, checking over his supplies.

"It looks like you've got most of what you need here. I would have made Jakey pack a hat, since it can get a little chilly there at night, and maybe one of those solar-powered backup chargers, just in case you wear out the battery on your phone. But it probably won't matter, since you'll have a bunch of other people there to keep you company until it's time to go to sleep."

She held out her hand for his phone. "Here, let me charge your phone while you finish getting packed. Though I'm not sure how much good it will do if you want to make a call. You're probably not going to get great reception out there."

Max handed over his phone but gave her a quizzical look as he did. "So you've done this before," he said. "Camping in Escalante?"

Pru nodded. "In Escalante, in Arizona and nearly every campground in Las Vegas. Jakey was in the Hiking Club, and I tried to chaperone all of his field trips."

Max looked at her as if she'd just grown another head. "Why?"

"Why?" she repeated with a quizzical look of her own. "Because I love my brother."

"Sure, but you live in one of the best school districts in

Las Vegas. There had to be other people willing to chaperone on camping trips. Why would you, a single woman in her twenties who used to work nights, choose to spend her free time camping with a bunch of kids?"

Of course he didn't understand, Pru thought as she connected his phone to the charger on the nightstand. "You still had parents when you were Jakey's age, so you can't understand."

The conversation was becoming personal. More personal than they'd ever gotten before, and she expected him to quickly change the subject. But instead, Max said, "Try me. You'd be surprised at what I'm capable of understanding. My parents are still alive, but they haven't exactly been there for me either."

No, they hadn't. Coleridge Benton II, the dad Max and Cole shared, hadn't even bothered to show up at Cole and Sunny's wedding. According to Sunny, who'd met him only once, her seldom-seen father-in-law was a bit of a Peter Pan, still roaming the world and refusing to grow up. Actually, she hadn't called him a Peter Pan. Her exact words had been, "Like Max. He's a lot like Max. More interested in having fun than relationships."

"Yeah, that's actually kind of why I had to go," Pru answered, continuing to fiddle with the charger. "Our dad— he was great. A teacher. The kind of guy who would have volunteered to go on camping trips with Jakey. So I went in his stead. It wasn't the same, but at least Jakey knew he wasn't alone in the world. He had me. Maybe it wasn't enough, but it was something."

She went quiet then, feeling silly for having told a guy like Max even that much. It didn't help when she looked up from the charger and found Max openly staring at her. In that way of his—the one that made her feel completely naked and exposed, even when she was fully dressed.

"If you only have twenty minutes, you should finish packing," she mumbled.

Max just kept looking at her. "Does he know?" he asked.

Pru shook her head, confused. "Know what?"

"What a good big sister you've been to him," he answered. "Does he appreciate that?"

The question made Pru's stomach lurch, and his steady gaze felt raw on her skin. He had no idea what a poor substitute she was for Jakey. She'd never be able to make up for what he'd lost.

"Let's not talk about Jakey," she said.

She went over to the desk and picked up the sketchbook he'd left there. "You should take this, too. It'll give you something else to do tonight."

Max took the wire-bound pad from her with an irritated look.

"C'mon, Max, I know it's not what you're used to, but it won't be that bad. Escalante is beautiful, and camping isn't the worst way to spend a night here in Utah, trust me."

Max zipped the backpack with a jerk of his arm. "I'm not angry because I have to go camping. I'm angry because I wanted to spend the night here. With you."

Pru's heart stopped. Was Max trying to say he was going to miss her? That he was angry about the unexpected trip, because it meant they'd have to be separated?

For a moment, she was actually touched. But then he said, "I still have eighteen wallets to cash in, and we only have a couple more days left here."

The wallets. Of course that was why he was really upset. Max might be better in bed than the guys she used to date, but that didn't mean he thought of her any differently.

This was what made Max so dangerous, she thought. One minute he was giving her undeserved compliments for chaperoning Jakey's camping trips. The next he was reminding her that she was his current plaything.

Pru didn't know why her heart shrank with disappointment then. Max had never claimed to be anything but exactly what he was. A wolf in designer jeans.

"Have fun on your camping trip, Max," she said with a thin smile.

Then she went back to her computer, not knowing whether to flip him off for blackmailing her into the wallet agreement or thank him for this not-so-subtle reminder that Max Benton really wasn't a good guy.

Chapter 17

Why Cole had decided to drag them all out to a campground in Escalante, Max still had no idea. Cole started the surprise excursion off with a little speech about the future of the Benton Inn, but it wasn't exactly a halftime game changer. First, he reported that the Benton Inn's opening would be delayed by a couple of months due to an unexpected bedbug infestation that would require them to replace quite a few beds and much of the carpeting.

"It's a tedious and expensive setback," Cole told them, "but we'll take care of it and the Benton Inn will open right before Thanksgiving."

Then he sat on a log and gave the floor to Gus and Harrison. Well, actually to Gus and his satellite smartphone, which Harrison used Skype to call in from, having bowed out of the trip due to his ankle. Gus did most of the talking, but Harrison chimed in every once in a while with numbers he apparently had pulled up on a computer, since they couldn't exactly have a PowerPoint presentation out there.

Max had to give it to Gus. The updated presentation wasn't half-bad. Gus announced they were in talks with a DJ who was on track to break big the following year, but open to residency while he put his first album together. They'd also decided to interview a few more design teams for the renovations and, after running some numbers, had decided to add two of the four cities Max had suggested to their East Asian ad campaign. Gus might not have the best initial instincts when it came to marketing, but he corrected well, and he knew how to deal with the hotel's more mundane day-to-day business. There were still a few more issues Max could have raised, but he didn't. Mostly because he wasn't exactly in the mood to give any more helpful advice to the guy who'd made such a brazen run at his wife that morning.

His wife for now, Max corrected himself. And for the first time he wondered what would happen after he and Cole signed his trust papers. Once Pru was a free agent again, would Gus swoop in? Max felt his nails dig into his palms, and he looked down to see that both of his hands were now fisted on top of his knees. He shook his hands out and forced himself to think of other things, not liking how dark his mind went when he thought of Pru going for Gus after they put in for a divorce.

Max was miserable for the rest of the day. And not because he was camping. Prudence had been right. It hadn't been so bad. He and Cole had won the unofficial fly-fishing contest, their combined general competiveness netting more fish to throw back into the stream than any other team. And he would have put the Dutch-oven stew the execs were forced to make in yet another team-building exercise up against any gourmet meal he'd had in five-star restaurants around the world. He couldn't even really complain about the two presentations he'd been forced to sit through.

As it turned out, the life of a hotelier on executive vacation suited him. And as much as it should have annoyed him that Cole insisted on keeping him close by his side, he had to admit that watching Cole work over the past few days had been good for him.

Max was a big-idea guy, while Cole's vision, like their Granddad's mission statement, could be summed up in four words: More Hotels, More Money. But seeing how Cole put together the details of launching a new hotel outfit had served to further inspire Max in his own venture. He'd worked out every aspect of building and marketing his boutique hotel—the licensing, the building, the design and the marketing plan he was sure would draw in the tourists and locals alike. But working with Cole and the other execs had helped him see that he needed to put more thought into the day-to-day management of the place. As annoying as Gus was, Max had to admit, he'd been a damn good general manager in New Orleans—and those didn't exactly grow on trees.

Max was actually learning a few things on this trip. Learning and not minding the free business education. When they split for the night, going into their individual tents, he was glad Pru had convinced him to charge his phone a little more. He couldn't type new ideas into it fast enough.

He thought back to earlier that day when he'd gone fly-fishing. He'd found himself wondering whether Pru had ever done this activity with her brother. He'd nearly gone for his phone to call her before remembering he didn't have reception out there.

When he'd been eating his Dutch-oven stew, he'd wondered what Pru was eating. Had she decided to go into the small town of Escalante herself? Maybe bring Harrison something back? Harrison had mentioned her offer to let him use their shower during the team lunch that afternoon. He wouldn't be surprised if Pru made sure he got dinner, too. As tough as she tried to come off, she was just that kind of woman. The kind of woman who took care of others when she could.

After he was done typing all of his new ideas into his phone, he found himself scrolling to her name on his contacts list. He resisted the urge to press it, even though he had no service out there.

Not enough...

Disgusted with himself, he set the phone aside and brought out his sketchbook and began drafting out new plans for his hotel's casino floor. Ones that took into account everything he'd learned over the past week.

This thing with Pru was a means to an end, he reminded himself. And since he couldn't currently cash in a wallet, there was no reason to call her. Even if he was feeling weird about the way he'd left things with her before departing their room at the lodge. She'd looked so disappointed when he mentioned the wallets. As if she regretted opening up to him even the little bit that she had. As if Max was scum she had no business associating with.

Not enough...

The words echoed in his head, refusing to stop, even when Max added *yet* out loud. When he got back to the lodge, he'd spend the next two days making sure he got his fill of Prudence. By Friday she'd be out of his system. And by Saturday he'd be back in New Orleans, putting his plans in place for his hotel.

"Son of a..."

He shook his head at his sketchpad. Somehow his new casino floor had sprouted a nose, a pair of dark eyes and a set of full lips that looked an awful lot like his temporary wife's features.

"Hey, Max," Pru's voice whispered. "Don't be afraid, it's just me."

His tent door was unzipped, and then Pru herself crawled inside the space like a vision called up by his unintentional drawing.

Max blinked, wondering if his weird obsession with her had ramped up to hallucinations.

"Hi," she said, rezipping the door before taking what looked like a new camping backpack off her shoulders.

She set the backpack on the ground in front of her and pulled out a stainless-steel thermos. "I brought you some hot cocoa," she whispered. "It always helps Jakey get to sleep on camping trips."

Okay, well that sealed it. Max closed the sketchbook

on the drawing he'd accidently made. If she was just a fig-
ment of his fantasy, she definitely wouldn't be giving him
hot chocolate or mentioning her little brother or be clothed
for that matter.

And for once she was wearing regular clothes. What
looked like a pair of sweatpants made within the current decade and a long-sleeved Henley worn under a padded vest.
She looked…adorable. Like one of those ads for camping
that the Vegas Tourism Board sometimes ran to convince
out-of-state tourists that there was more to do in Vegas
than party and gamble.

Max accepted the thermos she was holding out to him
and took a careful sip. It was insanely good. Even better
than the Dutch-oven stew.

Pru grinned when he looked back up at her in amaze-
ment. "Dark chocolate, two squares of a milk-chocolate
candy bar, honey, whole milk and a pinch of sea salt. It was
my mom's recipe. Guaranteed to put even the most terrified
kid to sleep on a dark and spooky night. You're welcome."

He took another sip, wondering what it was like to actually have good memories of your mother, as Pru did.

"What I'd do to deserve your hot chocolate?"

It hadn't been meant as a sexual innuendo, but once it
was out of his mouth, he could see why Pru took it that
way. "Absolutely nothing," she answered, her voice as dry
as the canyon they were currently occupying. "But I felt
bad for you, so I decided to come out here and make sure
you were doing all right."

Max took another sip of hot chocolate and grinned at
her. "So you missed me."

She just shrugged. "I figured it would help with our
cover story if it looked like I couldn't be away from you
for even a night."

"How did you know this was my tent?" he asked.

"Nearly everyone else on the executive committee is
married or has kids or both. It's one in the morning. I fig-

ured the tent with the flashlight still on was either your tent or Gus's."

His hands tightened around the thermos. "What would you have done if it had been Gus's?"

"Apologized and told him I was looking for you," she answered. "I'm not an idiot, Max. I know how to keep up a cover story."

With an annoyed look, she reached for her backpack and pulled out a sleeping bag. One that she unrolled about as far away from his as she could get in such a small space.

"Pru," he said. "Come on."

She ignored him.

"Come on," he said again. "You can sleep over here, with me."

"This sleeping bag will do me just fine," she assured him, smoothing out its wrinkles.

"Pru…"

He gritted his teeth, not believing what he was gearing up to say next. But it was late, he was tired…and it was true. "I missed you. A lot of the reason I'm still up is because I've been thinking about you all day. Can you come over here, please? Let me hold you."

Pru's back stayed rigid for a few more seconds, making him wonder if he'd have to invoke the wallets again. But then her shoulders sagged. "I guess," she mumbled. "It really does get cold here at night."

It wasn't that cold. Probably in the sixties. But he didn't argue with her. Didn't argue with himself. Just solemnly helped her rearrange the sleeping bags, laying one out on the floor of the tent and the other on top as a blanket.

He let her get into their makeshift bed first. Then he turned off his flashlight, letting the tent go pitch-black, before climbing under the covers himself. His mind, which had been looping around frantically, refusing to let him sleep, settled down as soon as he pulled her into his arms.

As if Pru was the answer to a question he didn't even know he had.

"How's the case coming?" he asked. Mostly to take his mind off the fact that lying like this with Pru felt better than the best sex he'd had with other girls in years past.

"Slow," she answered. Her body was stiff in his arms, as if she were expecting him to accost her at any moment. "All the execs are pretty clean, which you'd have to be in order to work in such a high-stakes job. A few execs from the Southern states tithe, and Harrison even gives nearly 20 percent of his income to charity."

She grew quiet for a little bit, then said, "But I did find some more weirdness where Gus is concerned." She shifted to look up at him. "Are you sure your grandpa didn't have some kind of other personal connection to him? Like maybe he owed someone associated with Gus a favor?"

Max answered truthfully. "I don't think so, or else he would have told us he'd handpicked Gus in the first place. He used to always lecture Cole about tracking his favors, so that he knew how to use them to his best advantage. If Granddad handpicked Gus as a favor to somebody, he would have told Cole, and Cole said Granddad never mentioned him. Why? What did you find?"

Again the tent fell quiet. "Why don't you want to tell me?"

"Because the last time I told you something about Gus, you ended up using it against him as a weapon."

"You don't trust me."

"No, I don't," she answered, her voice frank. "I'm also not interested in providing fuel for the next shoving match you get into with Gus. It doesn't advance the case, and eventually he's going to become suspicious about why you know all this stuff about him."

Fair enough, Max supposed. "Fine, whatever you tell me, I won't bring it up to Gus."

"You promise?"

"Is my promise worth anything to you?"

She ran a hand over the long-sleeved T-shirt he wore, brought it to rest over his heart. "No, not really," she answered truthfully. "You're a total liar. You've already proved that on more than one occasion."

This was true, but Max didn't like how Pru's assessment made him feel. "Well, I guess you're going to have to decide whether to take another gamble on me," he answered.

As a few moments of silence passed, Max thought she might decide against telling him. But then she said, "Gus aced all his standardized tests. But he had terrible grades in high school and a record. A few suspensions for getting in fights and, according to a New Orleans cop friend of one of my Las Vegas cop friends, he was brought into the station a couple of times."

Max frowned. "He has an arrest record? And he got hired at the Benton Group?"

Despite its seedy reputation in some circles, the casino-resort industry actually had much stricter hiring standards than many other businesses in America. It was near to impossible to get hired at one with an arrest record, especially if you were working as close to the money as Gus had during his years as the Benton New Orleans general manager.

"No, he wasn't exactly arrested. Both times he was let off with a warning," Pru answered. "And he was under the age of eighteen, so there's no official record on him. It's possible that since he started out lower on the managerial totem pole, your Granddad decided against a deeper background check. And since you don't need one to get promoted, he was able to make it all the way to the the Benton Las Vegas without anyone finding out."

Hmm. Maybe. But Coleridge I and Coleridge III had a lot in common when it came to trust. Neither of them did so easily, and it didn't sound like his grandfather to handpick anyone without having him thoroughly vetted first.

"Even stranger than that," Pru continued on, "Cornell

was the only program he applied to. He wrote a pretty terrific essay, but still it's a little hard to believe that he only applied to one Ivy League school or that he got in with his grades and his suspension record. If he hadn't been a foster kid, I'd think..."

She trailed off.

"Think what?" he asked.

"Well, the only other person I've seen with grades and a high school record like that was...well, you."

Max flinched a little. But he didn't deny it. "Yeah, I got into a few fights during boarding school, a few suspensions, too."

"Yeah, I saw that. But you're wealthy, so of course you got to go wherever you wanted. Guys like Gus, though— they usually don't bounce back like that. And the two arrests with just a warning...it's almost as if he had a very powerful friend on his side. Someone like your granddad."

Max's eyebrows lifted. "You didn't know my granddad. But he wasn't the type to go out of his way for some kid with anger issues he barely even knew."

"That's what I figured, too." He could sense her frustration, even in the dark. "Seriously, I don't know whether to give Gus mad respect for overcoming what he did or some serious sketch points. He's definitely a mystery."

That he was, Max thought, deciding then and there that even if Gus turned out to be clean, he was going to do some more digging into the new Benton vice president himself after all was said and done.

"So how did things go on your first camping trip?" Pru asked. Apparently she was done talking with him about Gus, and he was all for changing the subject.

"Fine," he answered. "Turns out I'm kind of good at being rugged. Fly-fished. Cooked some. Had some good ideas about the hotel, too, thanks to Cole."

This was kind of nice, he thought. Talking with her about his day.

He could feel her smiling against his left arm, which she was using as a pillow. "You and Cole seem to really be getting along better these days."

Max shrugged. "We're never going to be you and Jake. But we've been doing this for a few days and no punches were exchanged, so that's a new record."

He expected her to laugh, but instead she grew quiet before asking, "Have you two always been like this? This antagonistic?"

He let a few seconds tick by, then he said, "Short answer, no. We both had messed-up parents. Our dad was never around. His mom offed herself when he was a kid, and mine…"

He tried to think of a way to describe how Terese Mera had been. A wildly beautiful woman with raven hair, she, like her older sister, had been raised in upstate California by trust-fund hippies of Spanish descent. But unlike her older sister, who'd married a supposedly good man from a good family, she hadn't rejected her parents' bohemian ways. In fact, she'd taken it even further, becoming a painter and traveling all over the world, living life without a permanent address. It should have just been a funny story when she ran into her brother-in-law at a ski chalet in the French Alps. Back then, his father had still been trying to fit into the mold of a Benton heir, and had come to France to hobnob with big rollers, who might later choose the Benton when they came to Las Vegas. But it hadn't turned into a funny story, just a sordid one. What was supposed to be a two-week vacation turned into six. By the time Max's father got back on a plane to Vegas to inform his family he no longer wished to play the part he'd been assigned since birth, Terese was already pregnant.

One look, his mother had told him once. One look was all it took for Cole II to decide that he didn't want to walk in his father's footsteps and that he no longer wished to be married to her sister.

For the first few years of his life, Terese and his father had flitted around the world with him and a couple of nannies in tow. But as it went with all of Terese's lovers, the relationship had eventually imploded and they'd gone their separate ways. Despite having a son now, Terese had continued on with her carefree gypsy lifestyle. But she'd increasingly started to leave Max places. With friends in Barcelona while she went off with a new lover. With the family of an ex-boyfriend in Rio while she spent the summer in Saint Tropez. Eventually Nora had told her that if she was going to keep on abandoning her child, to leave him in Las Vegas, with his grandparents, who could at least watch over him properly until he was old enough for boarding school.

He'd moved in with his grandparents when he was five. But in many ways the stability of his grandparents' home came way too late. By that time he'd already grown the chip he'd carried around on his shoulder to this day. And he'd already learned the hard truth about women. Either you left them or they left you.

His father had left Terese and she had left Max. For as long as Max could remember, his number-one rule had been "leave before you get left."

Which was why he had no business snuggling with Pru or admitting he'd missed her while they'd been apart.

"What's wrong?" she asked him in the suddenly silent dark. "You've gone quiet. And tense."

"My mom wasn't like your mom," he answered, his voice tight. "She was messed up."

The silence that greeted his announcement let him know that this was another one of those things that Pru already knew about him. "I imagine that must have been hard, growing up."

"It was fine," he answered quickly. "I'm fine."

"But you and your brother used to get along and now you don't," Pru pointed out, her voice soft.

Max shook his head. "It's stupid. But I wasn't the only one getting in fights in boarding school. If you'd looked into Cole the way you'd looked into me, you would have found out he had the exact same record. Better grades but the same record as me. Back when we were younger and attending boarding school out east together, we were actually best friends. But then I guess Granddad finally accepted that our dad wasn't ever going to step back up to the plate. He pulled Cole out of boarding school and started grooming him to take over the Benton Group."

"And how about you?" Pru asked.

He shrugged his one free shoulder. "I stayed behind, kept on being Max, and Cole basically became a replica of my grandfather. He got even worse after Granddad died, trying to bring me to heel, telling me what to do. Basically sucking the fun out of everything."

"And now you're planning to start your own hotel," Pru observed. "Is that some kind of revenge scheme?"

"No…yes. I don't know," he admitted. "I don't like thinking about the stuff I do too hard. I just do it. 'Cause I'm Max."

Pru grew quiet again, as if processing what he'd just told her. Then she asked, "So how did you go from partying like a rock star to pretending to settle down with me so that you could start your own hotel?"

Max thought for a moment. "I spent most of my childhood in hotels and other people's homes. As soon as I graduated from college, I went right back to that lifestyle. For a long time I thought I was destined to live life like my mom did. But a few years ago, these thoughts kept coming to me. Ideas for the kind of hotels I liked but on a smaller scale, so that nonwealthy people could enjoy them. I tried to ignore those thoughts, but eventually…"

"…you had to follow through," Pru finished for him. "That's kind of how it went with me becoming a private investigator. The other girls in the Revue would ask me to help with these tiny mysteries of theirs. You know, like is my boyfriend cheating, I can't find my family heirloom, I think I got taken advantage of in this deal—stuff like that. And I'd become totally obsessed with solving their cases. Like I couldn't stop until I solved them. And that's what gave me the idea of becoming a private investigator after I hit the Benton Girl cutoff age."

"That's not an official cutoff age," Max reminded her. "You could have kept dancing if you wanted to."

"Yeah, I know," she answered. "But I didn't want to. I loved being a showgirl at first, but then…"

She trailed off. But Max had read the report on her, and now he could finish her sentence the way she'd finished his. "Your parents died in a car accident and you had to take care of your brother. That's pretty hard when you're doing two shows a night."

She averted her eyes. "Not really. At least I had my days free to take care of Jakey. And since you have to slather on the makeup for performances, I never had to worry about the dark circles under my eyes."

"As the son of a woman who had all the free time in the world and couldn't handle raising me, I'm going to disagree."

"No, really. It hasn't been a hardship at all. Jakey's a great kid."

"Why do you do that?" he asked.

"Do what?"

"Deflect any compliment I try to give you about raising your brother. Why don't you think you deserve any credit for that?"

She shifted. "Because trust me, I don't deserve any extra credit for raising Jakey."

"Why not?" he asked.

"So it went well with Cole today. Have you given any thought to telling him about your plans to build a hotel in New Orleans?"

He saw exactly what she was doing, the way she'd deflected his attempts to get to know her better with an invasive personal question of her own. "Okay, if you don't want to talk about it, we don't have to," he said.

And because he, too, was sick of talking about his messed-up family situation, he said, "You know, I've never done it in a tent. You?"

"Sure, lots of times. That's one of the behaviors they expect from chaperones when they're escorting a bunch of kids with raging hormones on camping trips."

Max grinned. "So, no."

"No," she answered. He could practically hear her rolling her eyes in the dark.

They both went quiet.

"Pru," he said, "why are you here?"

"I told you…"

"Why are you really here?"

"Like I said, this is a good way to make sure—"

"Pru, don't lie to me. Don't use selling our cover story as an excuse. Not tonight. I need to hear it. I need to know you missed me, too."

Pru shifted again. "I'm here, in your sleeping bag," she answered, her voice small. "Isn't that enough?"

Pru scared him. The truth was Max had never been this terrified of a woman in his life. But he told her how he felt. "No. It's not enough. And by the way, I should have told you this on Monday. I like your new haircut. It's cute. It brings out your face, makes you look even prettier."

She froze, as if his words were a slap across the pretty face he'd just complimented.

"What exactly is this about, Max?" she demanded. "Cashing in wallets isn't enough? You want me to humiliate myself first, because that's your thing, right? Making women think they have a chance with you. Complimenting them. Giving them the best sex of their lives, then you dump them? That's your MO. That's how you ruin them for other men, right?"

She'd pretty much nailed his tactic on the head. Blow a woman's mind, leave her wanting more.

Pru must have sensed the truth in his nonanswer, because she let out a weary sigh. "Max, it's been a long day, and you're right. I could have stayed behind in the room, but I didn't. I'm here with you, in this sleeping bag. And yes, it was hard to be in the hotel room without you, and no, I couldn't sleep, okay?"

"Why?" he asked. Needing to know, but hating how much he wanted the answer.

"Because I missed you." She didn't sound happy about this little truth. "It's stupid. I know it's stupid…"

"You missed me," Max repeated, unable to keep a silly grin off his face.

Unable to stop himself from kissing her, or rejoicing when she stiffened only a little before kissing him back.

But then just as the kiss was about to take on more heat, she broke it off, her voice desperate and ragged as she said, "Can we not do the thing with the wallets? Can we just pretend that we're not both messed-up people with messed-up pasts? Can we just be normal tonight?"

He stroked a hand over her short hair, which he hadn't lied about liking. And for the first time since he'd started treating women like playthings, he wished that he was a normal guy, capable of conducting a normal relationship. For the first time, he actually wished he was more like Cole.

He leaned forward and kissed her again. Not as a tactic or a punishment, but because he wanted to. Because she was a very pretty girl. Because he liked her, and because he wanted to feel her lips on his.

Asking Max to cut out his lothario act was a mistake. A huge one. Pru realized this just a few seconds after his lips met hers again. This time when his mouth moved over hers, it was with tenderness as opposed to his usual brutal force.

Being kissed by Max like this turned her mind into a total doily, with thoughts of first kisses and soft music. Max's kiss felt the way she used to wish boys would kiss her, back when she was a cheerleader and dating a football player.

The football player had never seemed to know what to do with his huge hands. Kissing him had felt like kissing a can of beer. Like a chore that came along with being a cheerleader.

But kissing Max was unlike anything she'd ever known.

Tonight he smelled of the outdoors and a cooking fire. He tasted like the hot chocolate she'd made for him. And the more he kissed her, the more she wanted him. She couldn't get enough of him, and soon she was panting against his lips, pressing her body into his.

"Max…" she whispered.

She didn't have to say anything more. He moved away from her, and cool air hit her as he climbed out of their makeshift bed. She could hear the sound of his new backpack being unzipped, then some rustling. He then got back under the covers with her. Naked now, with a condom in his left hand.

But instead of putting it on quickly, and taking her roughly as was his wont, he took her hand and pressed it against his chest.

"Touch me," he said, his voice low.

It wasn't a request, but it also wasn't hard for her to comply. She found she wanted to touch him, too. She brought both of her hands to his chest, mesmerized by the feel of his hard body in the dark as he she ran them over his chest and down his rippled abs. She stopped when she hit the top of his shaft, which was at full mast, already straining hard against the back of her hand.

The quick intake of breath he took when her hand grazed

his sex emboldened her. Made her linger there, stroking her hand up and down his long length.

As her ministrations went on, Max's breath become choppy, coming out in short bursts, as if it was becoming harder for him to hold on. Which only made her want to please him more.

She slipped down underneath the sleeping bag's top hemline, and soon she had him in her mouth. This time it was Max whose hips bucked underneath her oral ministrations, his hand finding its way to the back of her neck. "Pru…" he called after a few minutes. "You're killing me…"

It must have been true, because a few seconds later, he sat up and pulled out of her mouth. Pru sat up, too, and watched him put on a condom, desire hooding her eyes.

She didn't get to enjoy the sight for long. Soon after, Max reached over so that he could slowly strip her naked. His undressing was an exquisite torture, his hands grazing but never lingering too long on her now highly sensitized skin. But the torture didn't last too long either. She soon found herself on her back, biting her lip as Max pushed into her.

After he was all the way in, he paused, one hand finding the side of her face in the dark. "So beautiful," he murmured gruffly, even though he couldn't possibly see her.

He leaned forward and kissed her soul deep, and only then did he start moving inside her. With strokes so deep and thorough that the top of his shaft kissed her throbbing button every time he thrust into her.

The way he took her this time didn't feel like taking. It felt like something else. As if he was making love to her. Not punishing her, or conquering her, but loving her body with every stroke of his.

Tears pooled in Pru's eyes. She'd never been made love to like this.

The orgasm came on without warning. Arching her back

as it crested over her in a wave so powerful it choked her, stealing every single ounce of air out of her lungs.

Max came soon after. His entire body thrashing once, before he pressed his forehead hard into hers, as if bracing himself against the same wave that had rolled over her.

Only then did Pru realize what a mistake she'd made by asking Max to play it straight tonight.

Maybe if he'd continued using sex as a weapon to manipulate her, she would have been all right. But this…this had been too much for her. And when Max rolled away from her, only to come back with his discarded T-shirt, which he used to dry her eyes, she understood what he'd done to her.

By playing the part of a loving man, Max had ruined her. Ruined her for any other man for what she suspected would be a very long time.

She wept then, shaking with knowledge.

"Shh…" Max's voice was in her ear now, his arms coming back around her as he pulled her close. "It's okay," he said, as if reading her mind. "It's okay. We're okay. Let's just sleep. We'll figure this out tomorrow. It's okay."

It wasn't okay. He had no idea. It definitely wasn't okay.

But eventually her trembling stopped, and she went to sleep anyway. After all, a fantasy made was a fantasy kept. Until you opened your eyes.

Chapter 18

"Max, wake up."

Max didn't want to open his eyes. He wanted to continue sleeping with his arms wrapped around Pru's soft body.

But she shook him and said it again. "Max, wake up!"

Max reluctantly opened his eyes, only to see that they were no longer in a tent, but in a large bedroom. No, not just a bedroom—but one located in a penthouse suite with large windows overlooking the Mississippi River and hyper-realistic wallpaper designed to look like antique wall moldings from Old World France. There also a bright red couch shaped in the form of a pair of lips.

A bright red couch Pru sat on with her long legs crossed and her arms spread. Her body completely naked except for the diamond ring on her hand, which glimmered in the morning light.

Max quickly sat up. This tableau looked just like a picture he'd sketched. One from the last time he'd spent a few nights in one of his favorite Parisian hotels, detailing what his personal suite atop his New Orleans hotel would look like. Was he really here? In his own finished hotel?

"You sure are, Max." Pru answered his unspoken question with a sexy smile. "You hungry?" she asked.

A silver breakfast service appeared on the low coffee table that sat in front of the couch. It was piled with food. Beignets and croissants. Fresh fruit and grits. Orange juice and fresh coffee.

His stomach growled. Though, whether it was because he was hungry for breakfast or for Pru was anyone's guess.

"You're starving." Pru crooked her index finger, drawing him forward. "You better come eat, Max."

He started to get up, more than ready to join her on the couch, but then came Pru's voice again, hissing, "Max, wake up!"

The Pru on the couch frowned, her eyes shadowing over with disappointment. "You should wake up," she told him.

"No." He shook his head. "I want to stay here with you."

But Pru shook her head, looking as sad as she had on their wedding night when she'd told him she wouldn't be there in the morning. "You can't stay here with me, Max. Wake up."

Max shook his head. Refusing to take his eyes off Pru.

And Pru suddenly rushed forward, shaking him. "Max, wake up! *Wake up!*"

Max's eyes flew open and he sat up, looking for Pru. His Pru, the one he'd just left behind in New Orleans.

But instead he found a fully dressed version of her, typing furiously on her smartphone with one hand as she shook him awake with the other.

"What's going on?" he asked. "What time is it?"

"Five a.m.," she answered. "And what's going on is that a New Orleans hotel blog just announced that the Benton Inn won't be opening in October as planned because they've got a bad case of the bedbugs."

Max shook his head. "But Cole just announced that yesterday. And we were all out here. How did a blog based in New Orleans find out about it already?"

"I don't know, Max," she answered. "That's what I'm trying to figure out. Also what I was supposed to figure out last night before the mole was able to use the info."

She shook her head with a self-directed baleful look. "But unfortunately, I let myself get distracted. And now I'm trying to figure out who made the call to Key Card before it becomes a national story and Cole fires me for coming up with this stupid plan."

At first Max didn't understand what she was talking about or how she was able to use her phone when they didn't have any reception out here.

And then he did.

He stared at her. "This—you coming to my tent. It wasn't part of the cover story. It was so you could be close if someone left the camp to get better reception and make a call to Key Card."

As plans went it was actually a pretty good one, except Max couldn't help but notice one detail. She hadn't told him anything about it.

"I'm on your list. You didn't tell me about the plan, because I'm on your list, too."

This observation made Pru look at him for a long, blunt moment before letting out a heavy sigh. "Max, you're a liar. You've said so yourself. And you're planning a rival hotel that you still haven't told Cole about. What kind of detective would I be if I didn't put you on the list of suspects?"

Max's entire body went cold. "I might be a liar, and I might be competition, but I wouldn't sell out my family's business."

Pru didn't answer. But she didn't have to. The way her eyes flashed told him everything he needed to know about her thoughts on his general character.

She shook her head and went back to her phone. "It doesn't matter anyway. You definitely didn't leak this. I can vouch for you, and no one left the camp last night, so someone must have snuck in their own satellite device…"

"You mean like the one Gus used to patch Harrison into the meeting through Skype video chatting?" Max asked with a frown.

Pru blinked at him. "Wait? What?"

Chapter 19

Pru needed to get into Gus's room. It was all she could think about after sneaking out of Max's tent and hightailing it back to the lodge.

She'd let Cole down. And the look on Max's face when he realized that he'd been on her list of possible suspects all along was painful to observe.

By the time the executives started arriving back from the campground, she could barely contain herself. Her mind was a mess—so was her heart, and it felt more imperative than ever that she solve this case and put some distance between her and Max.

From a perch at the top floor's inner rail, which overlooked the entire downstairs, Pru watched Gus walk across the open common area below to his downstairs room. He had a leather overnight bag slung over one shoulder. She had to find a way to get to the satellite phone Gus had brought with him on the camping trip. It was the only way to prove that he was the one behind the leak. And she had to do it sooner rather than later, because the longer she waited, the longer he'd have to get rid of the evidence. For all she knew, he already had.

"You look like you have a lot on your mind, young lady."

Pru looked up and found Harrison standing next to her in a bathrobe.

Somehow she mustered up a half smile. "Hi, Harrison. Did you want to use our shower?"

"If it's not too much of a bother," Harrison answered, nodding at the clunky boot on his left leg. "I'm told I'll have to wear this darn thing for at least two weeks. But I don't want to disturb you."

"It's no problem at all," she assured him. "I've already taken my shower and Max isn't back yet."

"Good, good, as long as I'm not being any bother." He peered over his glasses at her. "Are you sure you don't want to talk about whatever has you looking so pensive. I'm told I lend a good ear."

This time Pru didn't have to fake a smile. "I'm sure you do, but it's a little complicated—"

She stopped short, when she noticed Gus below, coming out of his room in a towel headed toward the common showers.

Pru's heart jumped. Now was her chance—maybe the only chance she'd get.

She headed toward the back stairs, calling over her shoulder to Harrison, "The door's open, just go right in."

She didn't wait for his response, just hightailed downstairs, hoping that she had what she needed in her purse to make use of her extremely rusty lock-picking skills. But to her great relief, Gus's door was already open. She looked over both shoulders before turning the knob and creeping into the small room.

Gus's room was not what she expected, given his age and gender. No stray items floating around, every piece of clothing either hanging in the closet or folded in a drawer.

It was all very…regimented. Like the rooms of people who'd served in the armed forces. *Or like the room of someone who'd never had anything to call his own*, she thought.

A wave of sympathy passed through Pru. All signs were pointing to Gus as the most likely suspect in this case. But she already knew she wasn't going to enjoy proving he was the mole. Gus was a survivor, and she couldn't help but respect him for all he'd overcome even as she looked for the evidence to take him down.

However, that evidence didn't prove easy to find. She'd

opened every drawer, checked every pocket in his hanging row of suit jackets, but still couldn't find the satellite phone. And to her dismay, even the phone he'd left behind didn't give her much to go on. He'd reset the pass code—probably wise given the fact that it had been in Max's possession for thirty-six hours.

Her hand tightened around the phone, as she thought about just taking it. But that would be breaking quite a few laws—which could get the evidence declared inadmissible if the case went to court.

Meanwhile, there was one more place to look, and then she needed to get out of there quickly before Gus returned.

She went over to the closet, stood on her tiptoes and used her fingers to search its highest shelf. No phone, but what her hand did find brought a frown to her face as she grabbed a hold of it and brought it down to her eye level.

A sketchbook. A bit smaller than the one Max had, but it was also filled with drawings. As she flipped through the pages she saw what looked like possible design ideas for the Benton Las Vegas renovations that Max had mentioned in passing.

The discovery made her brow wrinkle. The vague hunch that had been only a tickle in the back of her mind before became a full-on gut twister, too insistent to ignore.

Research and guts. Guts and research. Other than her extensive list of connections, that was all she'd ever had to endorse her as a private investigator.

Feeling silly nonetheless, she looked around for something to prove her other theory and found it beneath the small mirror hanging above the dresser drawers. She grabbed the item and slipped it into her purse. Then she headed for the door.

Gus's room had been a huge bust. He'd obviously gotten rid of the satellite device, but maybe one of the back-end routes she'd set up to get into his phone was still available to her.

Pru froze in place when she heard the sound of footsteps approaching the door.

Oh no! Pru looked over both shoulders, desperate for someplace to hide. But unlike the closet in the master bedroom she shared with Max, the one in Gus's room was much smaller. Way too narrow and shallow for her to fit into. Under the bed was also a no go, thanks to its surrounding baseboard. Pru panicked, realizing there was nowhere to hide and no way to explain her presence in his room without possibly tipping him off before she got the evidence she needed to take him down.

Suddenly, a solution flew into her head at the very last second. In a haste, she ripped off the terry cloth polo she'd donned after her shower and dived. When Gus walked into the room, she was sprawled across his bed in nothing but her bra and a pair of seventies-era hot pants.

Gus froze when he saw her, his brow knitting for one confused moment. But then to Pru's great relief, his usual charming smile spread across his face.

Gus was a very good-looking man. And he knew it. Knew it and seemed to have no problem whatsoever believing that the wife of one of the Benton heirs would actually be in his room, on his bed.

"Well, hello there, Miz Pru," he said, closing the door behind him. "This is a pleasant surprise."

"Oh, I hope so," Pru said, playing along.

He walked farther into the room, his eyes roaming freely over her curves. "You and Max get into some kind of fight?" he asked.

"We had some words this morning," she answered.

Gus totally bought it. "I'm glad you did." He walked over to the bed. "Stand up for me, baby. Let me see exactly what you're offering."

He was bossy, she thought as she reluctantly crawled out of the bed to do his bidding. Like Max. But somehow not like Max.

With Max, she'd been embarrassed when he'd told her to put herself on display for him. But with Gus, it went deeper than that. A blood-curdling discomfort came over her that made her whole body feel stiff as she twisted it into a classic showgirl pose. Hands on hips, one leg splayed out in front.

It was a pose Gus responded to with a wolfish smile. "Nice. Tell me why you quit the line again?"

"It was time," she answered, since the real explanation of wanting to pursue her PI license certainly wouldn't help her cover story.

Gus shook his head and walked over to her. "Well, you definitely still have it. And if Max can't appreciate that, I definitely will."

He leaned forward to kiss her, and Pru tried not to react. But she...just couldn't.

"I'm sorry, this was a mistake," she said, ducking away from him, almost as soon as his lips touched hers. "I shouldn't have come here. I'm a married woman."

He looked down at her with a lazy smile and leaned in for another kiss. "I thought you and Max were having problems."

"Yes, a few," she answered, dodging the kiss. She hastily retrieved her discarded polo and headed for the door. "But this won't solve them. I should—I should go back to our room."

Gus shook his head, a bitter look coming over his face. "I get it. You like me, but why get with the vice president when you have a Benton heir? Even if he's an asshole who doesn't appreciate you."

His words made Pru stop at the door and turn back to face him, the polo pressed against her chest.

Her stare seemed to make him uncomfortable, and he unconsciously brought his hand up to his chest, rubbing his scar. The small gesture made Pru realize he wasn't a walking pile of testosterone with shady motives, but a man with feelings. Feelings she'd just hurt by offering him something she'd never truly wanted to give him.

"Actually, that's not it at all. I think…" She chose her words gingerly. "I think you're very impressive, Gus. Dedicated and hardworking. I really respect that, and the truth is, if I'd met you at the same time I met Max, I definitely would have chosen you."

This much was true. A stable guy like Gus, who'd spent his twenties working hard, as opposed to hound dogging through a series of women, would have been much more appealing.

"But, I'm married to Max now. So…" She trailed off, hoping that would serve as explanation enough.

Gus didn't answer her, just turned away with an angry sneer now marring his otherwise handsome face.

But this time Pru didn't stick around to hand out more comfort. She pulled the polo back over her head and opened the door—only to find Cole and Max on the other side.

She froze. Then scrambled to come up with a plausible story for being in Gus's room. One that wouldn't blow her cover. "Hi, Guys! I was um…just talking with Gus. What are you doing here?"

Max didn't respond. Instead he just stood there, looking down at her with eyes ablaze with fury.

But Cole, cleared his throat and said, "I see."

He nodded over her shoulder at Gus. "Gus, we wanted to ask you about that satellite phone you were using last night. I've been wanting to purchase one for personal use, and I was hoping I might be able to take a look at yours."

Pru felt Gus come to stand behind her, still only dressed in the towel he'd worn back from the shower. And she could almost see herself reflected in Max's eyes. Her shirt hiked up over her belly button because she'd put it back on so hastily, her short curls frizzy and ruffled from the action. A hot naked guy, standing directly behind her.

"The phone wasn't mine, actually," Gus answered Cole.

"I borrowed it from the lodge manager and I already gave it back to him. But I'm sure he'd be happy to let you have a look at it."

Pru's heart sank then, because it had actually been a pretty good idea on Cole's part for getting the phone, so that they could see what calls Gus had made on it. But Gus most certainly would have wiped the phone clean before handing it back to the lodge manager.

Pru took a step forward, hoping to extricate them all from the situation without being too obvious. "Okay, well, now that I've consulted with Gus about my issue, and you have, too, Cole, maybe we should go get some breakfast. I know you've got to be hungry after that camping trip."

"I am. Let's go eat," Cole agreed quickly.

But Max answered, "So you would have chosen him," the anger in his voice barely contained.

She opened her mouth, having no idea how to respond to this without blowing everything. "Max…"

"Yeah, sorry you had to overhear that, Max," Gus said behind her. "But look at the bright side, man. You win. Gold diggers will always choose you over me."

Pru gasped with indignation. Seriously? He was calling her a gold digger now, just because she refused to give it up to him?

However, she didn't have time to properly respond before Max was through the door, pushing past her. Apparently, he'd decided that Gus's heart condition didn't absolve him from anything because the very next thing he did was punch the Benton Group's newest vice president straight in the face.

Chapter 20

Max, having been born rich and ornery, had a basic rule about fights. Fights were fine. He had no problem with them whatsoever, but for the good of his bank account, it was necessary that he always made sure that the other guy threw the first punch. It just made things easier when it came to saving him from the consequences of getting into fights, like having to sit through a bunch of boring court proceedings. However, Max broke that rule with Gus.

Gus, as it turned out, was a pretty good fighter. He took the first punch like a pro. Then quickly raised his fists to protect his face before throwing one of his own at Max.

This definitely wasn't his first fight, Max thought as he deflected the punch and got Gus with an uppercut, straight into the gut.

Gus's grunt of pain was all the satisfaction Max got before Cole's hands clamped around his shoulders, pulling him away.

"Close the door!" he heard Cole tell Pru as he wrapped a restraining arm around his neck.

Max tried to wrench free, feeling an almost murderous need to wail on this guy.

"Max, calm down," he heard Pru say somewhere in the background.

"Yeah, Max, calm down, boy," Gus said with a half laugh, half cough of recovery from taking Max's gut punch. "Not my fault Pru likes me better than you. You can't buy everything."

"I don't like him better than you," Pru insisted. She

then appeared in front of him, her eyes pleading with him to believe her.

But he couldn't. Couldn't calm down. Couldn't stop hearing what she'd said to Gus. Couldn't stop seeing her in the doorway with her clothes all ruffled. How far had they gone?

He must have made an unconscious move to go after Gus again, because Cole's arm tightened around his neck, working even harder to keep him away from Gus.

"You're fired!" Max snarled at him.

"You can't fire me," Gus shot back.

"No, but I can," Cole said, his voice grim. "So how about if we call it even? I won't fire you for consorting with my brother's wife. And you won't sue us because he punched you."

Gus considered his offer and caved with a short nod. "Fine," he said to Cole. But then his eyes found Max's. "But you should know, man, she came to me. Not the other way around."

This time Cole wrestled Max out the door before he could respond.

The details got a little fuzzy after that. But less than a few minutes later, he was back upstairs in the room he'd shared with Pru. After she shut the door, she said, "You know that was just for the case. You know there's no reason for you to…"

But he could barely hear her over the sound of his own harsh breathing. Nor over the words, pounding red inside his chest: *Not enough…not enough…*

"You. Don't. Lie," he reminded her.

A troubled look came over Pru's face. "No, I don't," she admitted. "But—"

He didn't let her finish. He'd heard all he needed to hear.

"What are you doing?" she asked behind him.

"Setting a timer," he answered between clenched teeth. Then he locked in eighteen hours and pushed a few keys so that the countdown clock filled up her laptop's entire screen. "I want my eighteen hours. Right now."

I want my eighteen hours. Right now.

That was all the warning she got before Max was all over her. Ripping off her Henley, stripping off her bra. He pushed her back onto the bed and shoved down her hot pants over her legs. Disposed of without a care.

And then there was Max between her thighs, forcing her legs over his shoulders. His tongue hit her sex with such precision that she could feel the vibrations from its hard strokes all the way up to her womb.

Pru wanted to hold on. Wanted to stop this train and explain to Max exactly what had happened with Gus. Even though she shouldn't have to, because they were only fake married and she was only doing her job.

But his mouth was relentless on her sex. So deft in its actions that she could barely talk, much less tell him her side of the story.

"Max..." she groaned, trying to rally.

But then the first orgasm hit her like a train, starring out her mind and making her completely forget what she was about to say.

When her senses came back, Max was above her, flipping her over and pulling hard on the front of her thighs so that her butt was in the air, on full display.

There was a moment of savage silence, in which she could feel his burning gaze on her exposed behind. Then he leaned over her, his chest blanketing her back, his large hand cupping her sex from behind.

"Do you think you'd get this wet for Gus?" he asked her, his voice low and cruel in her ear.

He pushed three long digits into her tunnel. "Do you think he'd ever be able to make you come as fast as I just did?"

Pru bit her lip and shook her head, trying to fight a nearly overpowering urge to ride his hand.

"Hmm," he said above her. "You're fighting yourself again. Tell me, Pru, what makes you do that? Fight what you are deep down inside, what I bring out in you? Why can't you let yourself just ride my hand? You obviously want to. That orgasm I gave you couldn't have been enough."

It hadn't been enough, but she kept herself still, refusing to obey her body's instinct to push against his hand.

"All right, I guess we'll have to do this the hard way," he said above her.

His fingers started moving, pumping into her in a knowing way, as if Max was reminding her he knew how to please a woman. Knew, and was perfectly willing to use it against her.

"Tell me what happened with him. Exactly what happened."

"Nothing!" she gasped. "It's none of your business. But nothing happened."

"Nothing," he repeated. "Did he kiss you?"

She didn't answer. And he switched the position of his hand, so that his palm was on her clit as he pumped into her. Combined with the pressure of his heavy erection against her backside, the new angle nearly made her come again.

But she didn't. She just kept her body still as his hand expertly manipulated her core for what felt like hours.

Eventually Max growled. "Why are you still fighting me?"

She shook her head.

"Are you forgetting I know who you really are?" he asked her, his voice low and mean. "Did you let Gus meet Wedding Night Pru?"

The answer was no. She never let her out. Ever. Only with Max. But she remained silent. It wasn't as if Max Benton needed yet another woman proclaiming that he brought out things in her that no man ever had.

"Let her out now," he demanded above her.

"You want to hear the truth? Fine, here's the truth," she said, her voice ugly and raw. "Gus is boring, and stable, and all the things I've come to respect in a man since I became all those things myself. You, on the other hand, are spoiled, and rich, and truly messed up. So yes, if it had been up to me to choose before New Orleans, I would have chosen Gus. Because he's a halfway-decent guy, and you're a rich kid who thinks he deserves everything, including me."

His hand stopped, her assessment of his character effectively ending the conversation.

The next thing she knew, his fingers were out of her—now clutching her waist as he pushed himself inside her.

It was over quickly after that. After what he'd done to her with his fingers, Pru couldn't have stopped the orgasm if she wanted to. It ripped through her with the uncontrollable ferocity of a tornado, taking out everything in its path, including her dignity.

He pulled out, removing himself from her in one irate movement.

"That's one wallet," he said.

Chapter 21

Twelve wallets later, Pru came awake to a washcloth between her legs. Warm and wet, the feel of it both soothing and arousing her overworked core.

She didn't have to open her eyes to know what was happening. It was Max. Max sitting on the bed beside her. Max stroking her toward another orgasm while he cleaned her up from the last one. The one he'd prolonged until she was soaking wet in her own essences, begging him to stop, because she couldn't take anymore.

It wasn't the first time that night that she'd begged him. To stop pleasuring her, to keep on pleasuring her—all sorts of shameful things had fallen out of her mouth over the course of the past twelve hours.

At one point, he'd put her in a bath, she recalled now with no small amount of mortification. Watched her scrub herself clean with cool green eyes, then calmly reached under the water and put his fingers back inside her. Making her come yet again with a few calculations of his thrusting digits.

Then he'd let her sleep some more, waking her up sporadically throughout the day to make her come with his mouth or hand. Unable to resist, she had become more pliant as the hours wore on. She wondered if the hour would arrive when his touch didn't immediately set her on fire, eventually making her so wet that she climaxed again, even though she kept thinking she couldn't possibly have another one left in her.

But apparently she'd been wrong about that. Even now

she found herself responding to his ministrations with the washcloth. Whimpering as he rubbed her clean, stopping only to occasionally rewet the cloth in a bowl of hot water, until she came again with a full-body shudder.

"Thirteen wallets," he said, his voice monotone.

Pru opened her eyes then. She watched him put the cloth back in the bowl of water, get up and disappear into the bathroom. When he came back, he had two items she recognized in his hands. A tube of lip balm and her favorite body lotion.

It occurred to her to ask him what he was planning to do to her next, but the words stuck in her throat when she saw the size of his erection. Straining and hard as a battering ram. She stared at it, trying to figure out why he was doing this, why he'd decided to cash in all the wallets at once. He had yet to allow himself to come, even though he was obviously heavily aroused.

If he noticed her openly staring at his manhood, he didn't comment on it. Just sat back down on the bed beside her. She involuntarily clenched below, her body bracing itself for his intimate touch. But to her surprise, instead of traveling to below her waist, his thumb dipped into her tub of lip balm and applied it to her lips. When he was done, she instinctively rubbed her lips together as she watched him do another unexpected thing with his hands. He put a few pumps of lotion into them, rubbing them together, before he began massaging the extra moisture into her skin. First her legs, then her arms, then her torso.

His hands eventually made their way to her breasts, and she shivered. They ached now. From either what he'd done to them the night before or with anticipation for what he might do to them next, she couldn't say. Max had her mind and body turned inside out, so that she could barely tell which way was up or down anymore.

But his hands didn't linger on her breasts long. Instead, he pulled her forward, collapsing her against his shoulders as he massaged the lotion into her aching back. Despite the awkward position, it felt heavenly, like the best massage she'd ever received. And by the time he laid her back down against the pillow, her body felt supple and relaxed. Once again completely pliant and ready to receive his touch.

Max, however, inspected her naked body with the clinical distance of a scientist.

"You need to eat," he said, his tone grim. "It's late, but I can call the manager, have him bring up something."

He began to get up, but she caught him by the wrist. "No. No food."

He gave her an annoyed look. "I know you like to fight me on everything, but you're not going to make it through five more wallets without something to eat."

She sat up in bed, wincing at the many aches and pains the movement set off. "I'm not going to make it through five more wallets, period. The deal is off, Max."

He inclined his head, the angle making his jagged nose look that much more crooked. "So, good little Detective Pru has finally decided not to keep her promise?"

Pru was too tired to rally up much of a response to his dig. "Yeah, you wore me down. Congratulations, Max."

Instead of giving her one of his smug smiles, though, his face became hard. "The deal is off when I say it's off."

He leaned forward, and Pru shook her head, raising both hands to stave him off. "You're not getting it, Max. This is me, giving you what you really want. I'm saying you win. You've ruined me. The truth is you won Wednesday night, when we did it in your tent—that night you completely ruined me for any other man. You don't have to keep punishing me."

Max went still at her confession. But only for a moment. Then his jaw set and he said, "Five more wallets."

Had he not heard her? Pru began to snap at him, but then she realized… That's what he wanted her to do. He wanted her to be mad at him. He didn't want her to give in. He wanted a fight.

But Pru had no idea why. Though she did know what she needed to do next.

Knew and winced again as she moved over, making room for him on the bed.

"Max," she said. "We need to talk."

We need to talk.

Max went completely still. He'd had women say many things to him after he'd rocked their world. "We need to talk" had never been one of them.

"Five more wallets," he insisted through gritted teeth.

"Yeah, yeah, yeah, you're saying five more wallets and I'm saying we need to talk first." Pru patted the space she'd just created next to her. "C'mon," she said.

Max didn't move. He didn't trust himself to sit next to her without losing his mind and burying himself in her to the hilt. Didn't trust himself not to reveal how much power she had over him in that moment.

As if reading his mind, she asked, "Or are you afraid?"

Yes. Yes, he was afraid. Afraid of her. Afraid of what she brought out in him. Afraid of the obsessive words still ringing inside his head. *Not enough...not enough.*

But he moved to sit beside her anyway, wondering what she possibly thought she could say that would make him back down from collecting the rest of the wallets. He'd already skipped out on a whole day of meetings, texting his brother that both he and Pru wouldn't be available until Friday when it was time to sign the trust paperwork. Then he had turned the phone off.

"Let's talk about what happened with Gus," she said when he was settled in beside her.

"Nothing to talk about. I think you've proved who really turns you on over the past thirteen wallets."

It was a baiting tactic on his part. One she didn't fall for this time.

"Max, please, just…" she said with another wince as she gingerly scooted over and put more space between them, so that she could partially face him. "Just stop it with the lothario act. Let me talk for a little, please. I'm tired, and I doubt I'm going to ever be able to bring myself to do this again."

Max did as she asked, again wondering what she thought would convince him to give up on collecting the last wallets.

"What I said to Gus—you were right. It wasn't a lie. I would have chosen him a few weeks ago, because back then, I was lying to myself about who I really was. Telling myself that the woman you know as Wedding Night Pru was dead and buried. A few weeks ago, I would have dated someone like Gus just to prove she no longer held any sway over me."

Max shook his head. "That's what I don't understand. What's so bad about the person you used to be? Why do you act like she's some kind of monster who needs to be locked up? Like you don't deserve a little fun every once in a while?"

"Because…" She visibly swallowed. "Because she wasn't fun. She just seemed like a lot of fun. In actuality she was stupid, and petty, and a liar. My parents…they were really worried about her—me—I guess I should start saying me. My parents were really worried about me back then. I'd do things that I'd think of as living it up, and they'd end up having to come pick me up from some bar. Or spend their hard-earned money having to bail me out of some stupid situation."

Max blinked at her, stunned, and she nodded. "Yeah, surprise, I was kind of like you back in the day, Max. Wild, out of control, loved to party. I barely made it out of UNLV with my dance degree. The only reason I got hired for the

line was because my mom worked in the costume department. But even after I got a real job, I was only interested
in having as much fun as I possibly could. I worried my
parents sick, and I didn't care."

"In fact, I once skipped a whole week of work in order
to fly off to a tropical island with some trust-fund baby I'd
just started dating. Eventually I came to my senses when
he wanted to pass me around to a few of his friends—
apparently that's what he meant when he called it an 'exotic
vacation.' But I'd maxed out all of my credit cards, and I
didn't have enough money in my bank account to pay for
a last-minute ticket. So I ended up calling the parents in
tears. Told them I'd gone on vacation and miscalculated the
return date and missed my plane. And them being good
people—of course they bailed me out yet again. Used their
savings to buy me a last-minute ticket home. They even
asked a next-door neighbor to look after Jakey, so that they
could come to pick me up from the airport at four a.m. in
the morning—which is how they both ended up getting
T-boned by some guy who was driving and texting."

Of course Max had known about the car accident, but
his detective's report hadn't mentioned Pru's part in it. It
also hadn't prepared him for the guilty tears now pooling
in her eyes.

"If it wasn't for me, my parents would still be alive.
That's why I don't give myself much credit for taking over
Jakey's care. And that's why you don't have to bother with
proving that I've still got the old Pru inside me." Pru gave
him a rueful smile as she wiped away the tears. "Believe
me, I know she's still there."

When he'd started this journey with Pru, there had been
no doubt in Max's mind about how it would end. With Pru's
complete and total submission. Him the triumphant victor,
her the woman who would know now and forever that she
would never win in a fight with Max Benton—not even
an emotional one.

Technically her confession was the ultimate concession in their battle. She'd finally told him the truth about Wedding Night Pru.

But Max stared at her, feeling as if his heart was about to fall out of his chest, wondering if Pru knew that she'd just dealt him a fatal blow.

"Pru..." he whispered.

Pru shook her head. "It's okay. I just get a little emotional thinking about it."

"No, it's not okay. Come here." He had never in his life needed to hold a woman as much as he needed to hold Pru in that moment. He drew her now-stiff body into his arms, giving her the comfort he suspected she'd been needing for a very long time.

"Sweetheart, I'm sorry. I'm sorry about what happened to your parents. Sorry it made you want to bury the person you used to be. But..."

He tipped her chin up, needing her to look at him when he said, "I like you. *All* of you. Detective Pru and Wedding Night Pru. A lot. Too much actually. And it's driving me crazy. That's what this is really about."

She blinked at him. "You like me?" she repeated. Her tone was rightfully incredulous, given the things he'd said to her over the past thirteen wallets.

But he nodded anyway. "I really like you. That's why I can't see straight when I think about you and Gus. That's why I spent all day trying to prove to you, and to myself, that you liked me better than you liked him."

She gave him a watery smile. "Well, if that's all you were looking to prove, I can tell the answer right now. I don't like him. I could never like him the way I like you."

As warmth flooded through his heart, Max thought that this was what hope felt like. This was how it felt to like someone and hear for certain she felt the same way.

"You like me," he said, unable to keep a goofy smile from forming on his face.

"I like you," she confirmed with a shaky smile of her own. "I like you a lot."

She then snaked her hand around his neck and pulled him down for a kiss, one that tasted of the balm he'd applied to her lips.

When it was done, she gave him an apologetic smile. "But I've got another confession," she told him. "I haven't exactly been keeping up my end of the bargain, because the old Pru would have never let you get away with this."

As if to exemplify exactly what "this" was, Pru's hand came around his shaft, effectively switching their positions. Her the manipulator, him unable to keep from pumping himself into her fisted hand. She paused, but only long enough to run her palm over the top of his hood. His own thrusts became sloppy then, his whole body desperate for the release he'd been denying himself these many hours.

"Pru…" he choked out as his balls began to tighten.

But she suddenly released him from her warm grip and said, "So tell me about you. What made you the person you are today?"

He shook his head, confused.

Her eyes twinkled now, wicked with triumph. "C'mon, it's only fair. I told you about all my issues. You tell me about yours."

So…this was what it felt like to be on the receiving end of one of his own smug stares.

Max forced himself to play it cool. Instead of pushing her on her back and finishing as he wanted, he sat up a little straighter, lounging against the bed's headboard as if the raging erection between his legs wasn't an issue.

"You're the detective Cole hired to look into me," he answered. "Why don't you tell me? Prove you deserve the job in case I'm ever in need of a PI."

Pru studied him for a moment, considering. Then said, "Okay, fine. Here's my breakdown of Maxwell Benton."

She rose up and swung her leg over both of his. Making herself right at home as she sat on his lap with the lips of her silken folds resting right against the top of his shaft.

Max bit down. It was all he could do not to come from that movement alone.

"Let's hear it," he said, putting a whole lot of effort into sounding as if having her in his lap wasn't affecting him whatsoever.

"Okay," Pru answered…before wiggling her hips on top of him.

"Pru…" he growled. His fingers dug into her waist, anchoring her into one place.

"Okay, okay!" she said with laugh. But then she looked at him, really looked at him, her face becoming serious.

"So your dad was the first person to abandon you," she said quietly. "Then your mother left you with your grandparents, who sent you off to boarding school. So you formed a Brother Rebels Without a Cause alliance with Cole, only to have him abandon you when your grandpa pulled him out of boarding school and started grooming him to become the head of the Benton Group. And maybe that wouldn't have been enough to seriously mess you up. But then your grandpa died when you were in college. Before you could prove to him like Cole did that you weren't the screwup he thought you were. So you self-medicated for a long while, tomcatting around the world, ruining women before they could ruin you. And now…"

She gave him an empathetic smile. "Now you want to build a hotel. Partly to prove to Cole—who's basically become your grandfather—that you can, but also because you want to. Because it's in your blood and no matter what anyone else thinks, you know you'd be good at it."

Max froze, unable to completely process her words. Every single one of which was true. How could she have read him so thoroughly? He stared up at her in wonder.

And she gave him another rueful smile. Half shrug. Half apology. "Guts and research."

Guts and research.

Max continued to stare at her. He'd felt many things because of women. Horny. Annoyed. Challenged—at least for a little while. But he had never in his life felt the emotion that this woman had just inspired in him.

Understood. She made him feel completely understood.

"I like all of you, too, Max Benton," she whispered.

He needed to be inside her then. Didn't just want it or crave it, but needed it as he needed his next breath.

But he forced himself to be gentle with her. Lifted her up and angled himself, before bringing her down slow. Parting her folds as carefully as he could with his shaft.

He didn't want to hurt her, and he worried that she was too tender for even this gentle of an entry after everything he'd done to her the night before. But then she moaned with relief when he went all the way in, making him wonder if this—him inside her—was what she'd been waiting for, too.

Something would have to be done about this, Max thought later. Lying in the dark room, stroking Pru's soft curls as she slept with her head pressed into his shoulder. Poor woman. After what he'd put her body through, she'd barely made it through half the meal he'd had sent up before he'd had to remove the tray for fear of her passing out on top of it.

She'd fallen asleep nearly as soon as he'd tucked her head into the crook of his arm. Max was tired, too. Yet he remained awake, his mind racing.

He couldn't let her go. Whatever this thing was between them— Max broke off the thought as the L-word began to break the surface of his sleepy mind.

No, he couldn't let her go. Not yet.

He kissed the top of her head, thinking about the papers he'd be signing the next day. The ones that would absolve her from their marriage and allow her to divorce him without penalty.

He decided that when they woke up, the first thing he'd do was get her a huge breakfast. A substantial one that would make up for all the meals she'd missed over the past double-digit hours. Then they'd talk, really talk. About his future. Her future. And how they should be combined.

This decision made, Max finally allowed himself to fall asleep.

Chapter 22

When Max awoke next, it was to the sound of someone knocking on the door. A quiet but urgent pounding followed by Sunny's voice saying, "Pru? Pru, are you in there?"

Pru was already out of the bed, over by the closet, hastily throwing on a maxi dress.

"Coming," she called as she ran over to the set of dresser drawers. "Hold on."

She yanked open the top drawer, then threw one of Max's T-shirts and a pair of athletic shorts at him, hitting him square in the chest.

"Get dressed!" she whispered.

Max thought about refusing. He wanted to stay in bed with Pru. But Pru was already headed to the door, so he went along, getting out of bed and throwing on the shorts just in time to avoid being seen in his full glory by Sunny.

By the time he got his shirt on, Pru already had her arms wrapped around her best friend. At least she tried to get them all the way around Sunny. Sunny's substantial tummy got in the way of a full bear hug.

Pru pulled back and grinned at her friend's protruding belly. "Oh my gosh, Twin! You're so pregnant."

"Who are you telling, Twin? They barely let me on the plane back from New York with this belly. I was like, really, I'm not that far along. The baby just has tall genes. I thought I might have to ask Cole to send the company jet for me."

Max started to wonder why Pru and Sunny were calling each other "Twin." But then he vaguely remembered something from Pru's maid of honor speech about how the two were often mistaken for each other as the only two black dancers in the Benton Revue. And how they hadn't made it easy for the fellow dancers by wearing the exact same style of curly extensions.

As if to confirm the memory, Sunny gave Pru's short curls a surprised look. "You took out your extensions. I guess we don't look so much like twins anymore."

"End of an era." Pru grinned, trying to finger comb her tight curls back into some semblance of a style. "Sorry my hair is so messy. I rushed to the door. Are you okay?"

Sunny looked at Pru, confused, and Max walked over to stand in the doorway behind Pru and asked, "Why were you knocking on the door like something was on fire?"

Now Sunny's expression became apologetic. "Stupid pregnancy brain—I should have led with that. I was knocking because I wanted to talk to you first. Before Jakey got up here with the bags—"

Pru's eyes went wide. "Wait, what do mean Jakey? You didn't bring him here, did you?"

As if to answer her frantic questions, a male voice called out, "Pru!"

Then Pru's younger brother appeared behind Sunny. Even if Max hadn't already met him briefly twice, he would have known who the boy was. If Pru had about six more inches of height, a heavier jaw and, what Max was guessing from the ill fit of his T-shirt, a summer's worth of new muscle, she would have looked exactly like her younger brother.

"Jakey, what are you doing here?" Pru demanded. "You're supposed to be at camp!"

The teen answered Pru but glared at Max as he did so. "I left camp," he informed her, "when one of the other counselors asked me about you getting married to Max Benton in some wild nightclub video. Tell me that's not true."

"Jakey…" Pru clamped her mouth together. Max could almost see her mind working out an explanation that wouldn't technically be a lie but wouldn't blow their cover story either.

This current situation wasn't how Max had envisioned breaking the news to Pru's brother. He'd thought maybe they'd do this over tea or something at Nora's house when the young man got back from camp. But apparently this was happening now.

He stepped up and put an arm around Pru's shoulders. "Hey, Jake, man, I'm Max. Nice to meet you."

The teenager glared at him with the kind of prejudgment that would have served an old biddy four times his age. "I know who you are. Everybody knows how you do in Vegas."

He turned back to Pru. "Which is why I *know* you didn't really marry this guy, Pru. The video was fake, right? Like some kind of viral stunt ad or something for the Benton? Because he's way worse than all the stuck-up rich guys at my high school put together."

"Ah, come on," Max said, seriously offended. "You don't even know me."

"I know enough about you to be sure my sister wouldn't ever go out with a guy like you. Especially not without introducing you to me first. Not unless…"

Jake's eyes suddenly went wide and he turned back to his sister. "Is he paying you? Pru, is that it? Did he pay you to marry him?"

Pru tugged on his arm. "Jake, you're making a scene," she whispered. "Can you please just come inside so we can talk about this?"

Jake shook his head, refusing to be tugged inside, away from a now equally wide-eyed Sunny. "He is paying you, but why would you take money from him? Why would you…?"

Jake trailed off, answering the question before either Pru or Max had time to come up with a reasonable explanation. "It's because of BIT, isn't it? You're doing this for me."

The best thing Pru could have done at that moment would have been to deny it. To say to her brother, "No, of course not," and reiterate their cover story. That they'd fallen hard for each other in a matter of weeks and gotten married in a fit of heady romance.

But Max had called it right when he'd taken a gamble on Pru that first night with the wallets. She'd do a lot of things to solve her case and keep her promises. But he saw in those moments of silence that she didn't lie. Especially to her brother.

"Oh, my gosh," Sunny, who was still in the doorway, whispered. "Is this why you haven't returned any of my calls?" she asked. "Because you fake married Max and didn't want to tell me?"

Pru shook her head, her voice little more than a broken whisper when she said, "I didn't want to hurt you. I wasn't trying to hurt either of you. I just… I didn't think anyone would get hurt."

"I can't believe this!" Jake nearly yelled.

He pushed into the room, past his sister in order to grab Max by the front of his shirt and shove him into the nearest wall. "You paid my sister to fake marry you, and you made her…?"

He didn't finish that sentence. Just let his eyes scan the bed with its seriously rumpled sheets, before raising his fist, as if to tell Max what would happen if he didn't like his answer.

If it had been anyone else, Max would have baited him into following through. Goaded him into throwing the first punch, which he would have easily ducked before reversing their positions and showing the guy exactly how to land a good face punch.

But Jake wasn't anyone. He was Pru's brother. And Max really must have been out of his mind over this woman, because instead of showing Jake what real fighters did when you slammed them into walls, he raised his hands and said,

"Jake, I know you're mad. But I've never paid for sex, and I'm not going to go into the details with you. You need to trust that I would never force your sister to do anything she didn't want to do with me in bed."

Jake screwed up his face, his raised fist balling up even tighter. "Why would I trust anything that came out your mouth? My sister would never let a guy like you touch her. I went to school with guys like you. They made fun of me for being poor. We hate guys like you. A rich guy like you in a Lambo killed my parents. And he would have gotten away with it, too, if Pru hadn't proved the guy had been texting when it happened."

Max looked at Pru, who hadn't told him this part of the story, and his heart went out to her once again. He could only imagine the kind of guilt she must have felt over her parents' death as she went about solving the case of what happened to them herself.

"Pru…" he said, instinctively reaching for her.

But Jakey slammed him back into the wall. "She would never give somebody like you the time of day, and she damn sure wouldn't marry you for real without running it by me first."

"Jakey." Pru appeared behind her brother, placing placating hands on his shoulders. "Please, I know what this looks like, but I made this decision for a reason, and I know what's best for you and me. You've got to trust me."

Pru's words had an effect on Jake, but not the one she'd probably intended. He let go of Max in order to turn on her.

"Trust you?" he repeated. "Why should I trust you? Especially after you did this?"

Pru took a step back, covering her mouth with her hand. "Jakey…" she said, her voice filled with hurt.

"No, don't talk to me," he spat out, his face screwed up with disgust. "Just take me home. All I want to do is forget any of this ever happened. I can barely look at you."

"You can barely look at her?" Max repeated, grabbing

a hold of Jake's shoulder and spinning him around. "Are you kidding me?"

"Max, no!" Pru said.

Max ignored her, his eyes focused on Jake. "After everything she's done for you? After everything she's sacrificed? You think you have the right to judge her for any decision she makes?"

Jake didn't back down. "I suggest you get out of my face, man." Then he looked over Max's shoulder at Pru to sneer, "I can't believe you let yourself get mixed up with this guy. It's like the way you were before Mom and Dad died all over again."

Max didn't have to look at Pru to know that Jake might as well have taken out a knife and stabbed her.

With deliberate calm, he grabbed the young man by the front of his T-shirt and slammed him into the same wall he'd slammed Max against. Jake immediately tried to struggle free, but Max easily kept him there.

Somewhere in the distance, he heard Pru at his back, demanding he let her brother go, but Max stayed fully focused on Jake.

"Listen, dude, it's time for you to start showing your sister a little more respect," Max informed the younger man. "Yeah, she married me because she needed money to help you. She did that for *you*, and that means you don't get to judge her. In fact, the only words you should be saying to her right now are 'Thank you. Thank you for raising me, thank you for taking me on all those stupid camping trips, thank you for doing whatever it took to make my dreams come true.' That's *all* you should be saying to your sister now."

"No, Jakey, you don't have to thank me for anything!" Pru insisted behind him. "You deserve nothing less."

Max let Jake go. So abruptly, the boy would have stumbled backward if there hadn't been a wall at his back.

He let Jake go, not because of Pru's pleas, but because

he needed his hands to take Pru by the shoulders to look her in the eye. "Listen to me, Pru. Listen to me well. Your parents' deaths are not your fault. I understand why you've been blaming yourself all these years, but you've got to forgive yourself. And you can't let Jake or anyone else shame you into burying the real you again. Promise me you won't bury her, promise me—"

"Max." A cold voice from the doorway interrupted Max's desperate plea.

And Max cursed. Of course his brother, Cole, would choose that moment to walk in.

Chapter 23

Just when Pru didn't think the situation could get any worse, Cole happened. She stepped back from Max and watched his older brother take in the scene with cold eyes before deliberately walking over to his wife, Sunny. "Are you okay?" he asked, obviously struggling to keep his voice calm. "I nearly went out of my mind when Tomas told me you never showed up to let him drive you up here."

"I'm fine," Sunny assured him, rubbing his arm. "Jake showed up at the Benton, upset because he just now found out about Pru and Max, and I didn't want to inconvenience Tomas. So I decided to drive him up here myself."

Cole's face went hard with anger. "No, Sunny," he said. "I don't want you worrying about inconveniencing me or any of my staff. Especially now that you're pregnant."

Sunny looked up at him with soft understanding. "I know you're worried about me and the baby. But Pru's my best friend, and I love Jakey like family. You know that. I couldn't just turn him away."

That statement brought Cole's green eyes up to Pru. "Yes, I know Pru's your best friend," he agreed. "Which was why I trusted that this marriage wasn't a fake. I didn't believe she'd be willing to let my brother lead her astray."

Pru's whole body went hot with shame.

Sunny opened her mouth, but before she could defend Pru, Pru said, "No, Sunny. He's right. So is Jakey. I tried to justify it in my mind, but what I did was wrong, and I could not be more sorry."

Max, however, stared at his brother, completely remorseless. "What part of 'she did it for her brother' are you all failing to understand? She only agreed to this so that he could go to BIT," he told them.

Cole finally turned to address his brother. "She could have come to me," he answered. "Instead she chose to get tangled up with you. That doesn't say a lot about her character."

"Does Pru strike you as the type of woman who's looking for a handout? Jake was taken off the waitlist to BIT, and she wanted to earn the money fair and square. Keep her pride, even if it doesn't look that way from the outside to a clueless bastard like you."

Pru blinked, surprised that Max had read her motives for taking this deal so well.

"Keep her pride?" Cole said between gritted teeth. "On her back? With you?"

Max's whole body went rigid beside her as he clenched one fist at his side. "Sex wasn't part of the deal, and the only reason I'm explaining that to you is because Pru actually gives a damn about what you think of her."

Cole didn't back down from the challenge in Max's stance. In fact he came closer, standing nearly toe-to-toe with his brother. "So that's your story? Pru needed money so that Jakey could go to BIT, your very own alma mater. And he was taken off the waitlist exactly how long after you found out you'd need a wife in order to get your trust money?"

Now Max did back down, his eyes shifting away under Cole's hard gaze. The implications of what Cole was insinuating hit Pru like an anvil.

She shook her head at Max. "No, you didn't..."

But the defensive look in Max's eyes along with her own gut told her that was exactly what he'd done. He'd used his connections to get Jakey into BIT. But why?

"Max, there is no amount of money that would convince me to fake marry you."

"Never say never. That's what I always say when it comes to money. You never know when you're going to get hit with a rainy day."

Pru's stomach soured with realization. She hadn't been desperate enough to take his deal, so he'd decided to create a rainy day for her. She knew that now. As sure as she knew her own name. As sure as she knew that she'd been right to suspect there was more to Max than the reckless party-boy image he'd so carefully cultivated. He wasn't just a future hotelier, he was a master manipulator. Even better at getting people to fall in line with his business plans than his brother.

Before her mind could recover from the shock of her revelation, Jake sprung off the wall. Pointing an accusatory finger at Max as he said, "You rigged it. You rigged me getting into BIT?"

Max threw Jakey an uncaring glance. "Not exactly. You were high up enough on the list that I didn't have to rig anything, just make a few calls. You had the grades."

"What kind of person uses somebody's brother to get a girl to fake marry him?" Jakey shot back.

"The kind who knows his brother," Cole answered, his voice as dry as the Escalante Desert. "Max knew the wife he presented had to be someone I would buy. So he picked my wife's best friend."

Cole's eyes once again found Pru, but this time the hard judgment was gone. "You're pretty much the only person I would have accepted without at least a year of companionship, Pru. And apparently Max figured that out before manipulating things so you'd go along with his scheme."

Pru turned to look at Max, seeing him clearly for the first time. Seeing what a fool she'd been when it came to him. "So you did all of this…why? To get back at me? To get one over on Cole? Because you could?"

Other questions began roiling through her mind. Like why had he brought sex into it? Been so insistent about setting the wilder version of her free? And what about last night? When he claimed to like her in a tone so passionate, it had almost felt as if he was telling her he loved her? Why had he said and done all of that?

But she didn't ask those questions. She already felt stupid enough for letting herself develop feelings for him. Even though he'd told her what he was about from the first time they'd hooked up.

Max shook his head, his jaw tight. "Pru, I didn't set out to hurt you. I was only trying to—"

She slapped him, the sound of her hand cracking across his face reverberating through the room.

Then she waited for him to say something else, so that she'd have a good excuse to slap him again. But he didn't, just stared at her, his eyes hollow.

And in the silence that followed her slap, Pru heard Cole say to Sunny, "Honey, I need you to take Pru and Jakey downstairs. Give her your keys so she can drive your car back to Vegas. It's time for them to go home."

Chapter 24

Pru was aware she needed to get out of bed. And she would. Someday. Just not today.

When she cracked an eye open to find the Las Vegas sun already high in the sky, she knew it would be another day like the one that had proceeded it. One spent mostly in her bedroom, engaged in fitful bouts of gray sleep, trying to avoid her little brother during her occasional trips to their shared bathroom.

He'd refused to go back to his leadership camp after they'd returned to Vegas the day before. Even after she'd gone directly to her room and crawled into bed.

One more thing she'd ruined for him.

She'd let Jakey down. Him, and Sunny—the two people she cared about the most. Also, Cole, who'd given Pru her first two official jobs. All in the name of Max Benton.

I like you. All of you... A lot. Too much, actually. And it's driving me crazy. That's what this is really about.

The memory of his words continued to burn inside her. A raw wound that she hadn't been able to stitch closed even with lots of bad TV, sleep and the box of prebaked breakfast pastries she'd been subsisting on since Friday.

The once-full box contained only crumbs and empty foil packages now. But the memories of her last night with Max remained. *Why did he say all that stuff?* she wondered. He had made her believe that he really liked her, that he really wanted something beyond good times with her.

She'd never know, and meanwhile she'd get to live with those memories into the foreseeable future. She couldn't figure out what made her angrier, the fact that she'd been so thoroughly duped by Max or that she couldn't get him out of her head. Despite knowing how far he'd gone to make sure everything went exactly to his plan.

A knock on her door interrupted her pensive thoughts.

"Hey, what's up, Jakey?" she asked, sitting up in bed.

"Can I come in?" he asked on the other side of the door.

She looked down at the robe she'd fallen asleep in. "Sure."

Jakey poked his head in. "I was just wondering if you'd come with me to the storage place to work on the car."

Pru's stomach curdled with apprehension. Here it was. The moment she'd been dreading. The moment Jakey got up the nerve to ask her about Max and why she had slept with him, despite his slimy reputation, despite knowing from the start that he was a liar.

"Sure," she said to Jakey. She was able to keep her voice light, but she didn't even attempt to fake a smile, as she usually did when Jakey asked her to do something that she really didn't want to do. Instead she said, "Just give me a few minutes to take a shower and get dressed, okay?"

An hour later they pushed up the garage storage unit's rolling metal door together.

"So," she said to Jakey, feeling more than a little awkward, "what do you want to do today?"

They'd changed the oil and rotated the tires during their last visit. There really wasn't anything else to do. This was just an excuse for Jakey to get whatever feelings he was having about the whole fake-marriage incident off his chest.

Jakey headed over to all the materials they used to polish the Thunderbird's metalwork. "Figured we'd wash the car. Give it a really nice detailing."

"Okay…" she said, supposing that was as good of an excuse as any. "We haven't done that in a while."

They spent the next hour washing and polishing and vacuuming the car, until it gleamed under the garage unit's lights. But when they were on the last tire and Jakey still hadn't said a word about Max, Pru decided to address the elephant in the garage herself.

"So…what made you want to come out here and work on your car?"

Jakey didn't turn to look at her, but he did pause, his hand rag coming to a stop on his tire's decorative hubcap.

"I have a potential buyer coming by to look at the car in about an hour. Just wanted to make sure it was in the best condition possible."

Pru stopped polishing herself. "What do you mean you have a buyer?"

"I mean I posted the car on Craigslist yesterday and someone came back with an offer. A good one, about five thousand dollars above my asking price. So I'm going to sell it."

She stood up now, shaking her head. "You can't sell this car!"

"Why not?" he asked. "You're always saying it's really mine, because Dad would have wanted me to have it. You got Mom's clothes and I got Dad's car. I thought that was the deal."

"It is, but…" She struggled to find the right words. "Why would you want to sell Dad's car?"

"Because that's the only way we're going to have enough money to send me to BIT. And, I guess your boyfriend was right. He might have pulled a few strings, but I think I'll be all right there, able to hack it with the big brains. Plus, I've been thinking about all those rich kids at my school. Not the smart ones, but the dummies. The ones going to Ivy League schools because their parents made a big donation. Max didn't make a donation to get me in, but he made a few calls, so why shouldn't I take the spot? I deserve it."

"That's true…but this car is your legacy. I can't let you sell it because I didn't come through on the money side—"

Jakey interrupted her with a grim look. "Yeah, actually you can, sis. I've been thinking about what your boy-friend said…"

"He's not my boyfriend," Pru said, ignoring the pang of sadness that pierced her heart when she said those words.

"Anyway, I've been thinking about what he said, and some of it's true. I've been leaning on you too much, let-ting you do all the work. I didn't even get a summer job this year, because I just figured you'd take care of every-thing, like you always do."

"That's okay," she insisted. "I'm glad you didn't get a summer job. I'm glad you were able to finally be a coun-selor at your camp."

Jakey shook his head.

"No, sis, it's time," he said. "It's time for me to step up and be a man, stop depending on you. Stop acting like you owe me something, because Mom and Dad died. It's like this…"

He took a deep breath and said, "Sometimes bad things happen to good people. That happened to be their time, and that's not your fault. I don't want you to carry that anymore."

Pru wrung her hands, knowing it would take some time before she could truly agree to Jakey's sentiment.

"Okay," she said carefully. "I'm going to try to work on not carrying that, but I can't let you sell this car. I'll figure out something else. Take out a loan if I have to. You de-serve to go to BIT. It was Dad's dream."

"It's my dream, too," Jakey said quietly.

"What?"

"I'm not just doing this because Dad wanted me to go. I'm doing it because I want to go to BIT. I like math and science and I want to go somewhere with some of the great-est math and science brains in the world. Who knows, maybe I'll become a mechanical engineer and design a Thunderbird update that doesn't suck. Talk about living out Dad's dreams."

Pru laughed, remembering how their father had railed against every iteration of the Thunderbird put out after 1983. Jakey becoming a mechanical engineer with a mind toward car design would definitely garner him a few heavenly smiles from their father.

Jakey took her by the hands. "Seriously, sis, I want to do this. For me, not just because it's what Dad would have wanted. And I think it's time you started living your life for *you*, not for Mom and Dad."

She shook her head. "Jakey, why are you acting like I'm this huge martyr? You deserve everything I've done for you. *Everything.*"

"How about what you deserve?" he asked. "I'm pissed it took some rich guy to show me how it's been for you. How you haven't let yourself have a life because you were trying so hard to make me happy."

He pressed a hand to his chest. "I'm happy, sis. I should have told you that a long time ago. Yeah, it hurts not having Mom and Dad here, but I'm really happy. Because of you. And now I want you to be happy, too. It's not like Mom and Dad hated the girl you were back then. They were just worried about you. They wanted you to be happy, too. Just like I do. So let me sell this car. Let me be a man."

Pru, who had always had a hard time denying her baby brother anything, even before their parents died, suddenly found herself swiping at tears. He was right, she realized. He had grown up. He was becoming a man, and now their relationship was entering a new phase. One that would require her to start letting Jakey fight his own battles, and take care of himself.

"Okay, Jakey," she said softly. "I think I can do that."

"Good," Jakey answered. "Also, I'm going to need you to start calling me Jake, because this Jakey stuff isn't going to fly at BIT."

"Okay, *Jake*," Pru answered with a roll of her eyes. "Tell me some more about this buyer."

Jake shrugged. "Just some old guy who likes cars," he answered.

The "old guy," Pru found out thirty minutes later, turned out to be a distinguished older man from one of the most respected auction houses in the world.

"James Market. So nice to meet you," he said, handing both of them dark blue business cards.

James spent the next twenty minutes inspecting the car with a rather somber expression, only to break into a smile when he came back to join them outside the garage.

"Very nice, very nice," he told them. "Very well kept up. Our client will be happy to pay the agreed-upon price."

"So you're not going to put it up for auction?" she asked. She thought of all the reality shows she'd seen about buyers going around the nation trying to find treasures to auction.

"Oh, no," James said with a little titter, as if she was making some great joke. "We have people in other divisions who handle item procurement for the house. I'm an automotive specialist and simply here to broker a deal for our client."

"Who is…?" Jake asked.

James lowered his eyes. "I'm not allowed to say."

"Is it Cole Benton?" Jake asked. "Because if it's him…"

"…we know Cole, and we don't want to take advantage of his generosity," Pru explained to James. *Any more than I already have*, she thought, cringing anew at the memory of the way he'd looked at her when the truth about her and Max's marriage surfaced.

"It's not Cole Benton," James assured her. "I'm allowed to tell you that much."

"Or Sunny Benton? Or Nora? Or Max?" Jake asked.

Although why he thought Max would give a fig about them or their car, now that he'd lost his trust money, was beyond Pru.

"It's no one associated with the Benton family," James answered. "Now, are you still interested in selling?"

Jake shook James's hand. And they quickly arranged a time for Jake and Pru to come by the Las Vegas office that afternoon to sign all the paperwork and hand over the keys.

"Congratulations," he said to Jake after that first bit of business was all done. "I'm very glad this worked out for both our client and you. You don't see cars this well maintained often. Many times I'll think I've come across an auto that seems perfect on the outside but doesn't hold up upon closer inspection…"

Their car talk faded to the back of her mind as an idea suddenly occurred to Pru. An idea about wolves in lambs' clothing. An idea about the case.

It was entirely possible, she thought, that she'd been going down the wrong road with Gus. Maybe someone else in the Benton Group was the saboteur. Someone she never would have guessed, because he looked too good on paper.

Guts and research. Her instincts came back online with a ferocious roar, pushing Pru harder than they ever had before to follow up on her latest hunch.

Chapter 25

I'm over Pru, Max thought as he walked into his epony-mous nightclub. *All the way over her.*

He decided this after nearly an entire Friday and Sat-urday spent moping around his grandmother's mansion, wondering why he was still in Las Vegas. Why he hadn't been able to bring himself to return to New Orleans after all that had happened in Utah.

Despite all the sleep he'd gotten over the past couple of days, he was still tired. Tired of replaying his last scene with Pru in his head. Tired of remembering the hurt that had flashed across her face, before the disgust had set in.

She'd looked at him as if he was garbage when she slapped him. Probably because he was garbage. Always had been and always would be.

And then she'd walked away without a backward glance.

But whatever, he thought now. It didn't mean anything. Only that he must have gone temporarily insane to think even for a few measly hours that he and Pru had something more substantial than a one-week fling going on.

That bout of temporary insanity was done now, and he was back. Dressed in an on-trend lightweight suit that was nothing like the business ones Cole had forced him to wear in Utah. Headed toward the VIP section of the night-club like a king on his throne. Two, maybe three drinks, and he'd be all the way over Pru and her all-seeing eyes and her stupid understanding. Who needed to be under-stood anyway?

He dropped onto one of the white couches in VIP, and

bottle service magically appeared without him even having to ask. A few friends he had known from various party circuits had also made their way to the VIP area. That crowd, he'd noticed as of late, was starting to thin out. Coming out only occasionally for paid gigs, because they'd spawned or gotten into relationships that took up more and more of their time.

Because they'd grown up.

He remembered then the conversation he and Pru had had that last night together. The one that made it seem as if they were on the exact same page in life. Over their old ways, and looking forward to moving into a new phase. Sometimes he thought about settling down and starting a family like Cole and Sunny. More and more lately.

Whatever. Max threw back an entire flute of champagne and held out his glass, knowing someone else would fill it up for him.

Here's what he needed, he decided as he drained another flute of champagne—a girl, someone smoking hot, to help him forget all about Pru.

"Hi, Max!" a set of high-pitched voices said in unison.

Max looked up from his seated position to see two girls, one brunette and one blonde. They weren't in costume, but they had that familiar long-legged look of a showgirl. He vaguely recognized them from the Benton Revue—not the ones who did special performances all around town, representing the Benton, as Sunny and Pru used to, but the ones who went topless on stage.

"We just got done with a show," one of them said, "and we heard you were over here in VIP."

"Want to party?" the blonde asked, a bit more direct than her friend. "We know you Bentons really like showgirls."

She glanced at the wedding ring Max still hadn't gotten around to taking off. If she was concerned about it, it didn't show in her inviting smile.

Max grinned at them. Yeah, he was definitely back.

* * *

Less than three hours later, Max found himself leaned up against the jamb of a nondescript beige door, impatiently punching his finger into the doorbell embedded in its left frame.

When that didn't garner an immediate answer, he started pounding on the door with the side of his fist. Memories of what had gone down that night still burned in his head.

Two girls, naked on top of a hotel room bed, pretty and more than willing to let him have his way with them. He'd been able to get the same suite that he'd shared with Pru the night they'd been married, and it had been the perfect setup to scrub his mind clean of what had happened there.

He wouldn't call the the Benton Revue Girls snobs, but they were a proud folk. And most of them were pretty adamant about not being bunched in the same class as strippers. Every Benton Girl, including the nudes, had dance degrees and/or some kind of formal training. And they weren't expected or encouraged to fraternize with the show's patrons beyond the stage.

However, these two girls were A-OK with stripping for him. They put on quite a show, dancing to their own sexy inner music as they peeled off their minidresses. Then they kissed each other with a cunning ardor designed to both titillate and compel whoever was watching to join in on the action.

It should have worked.

Would have worked on him just a few weeks ago. But watching the two Benton Girls go at it had only served to make him think of what he didn't have. *Whom* he didn't have.

The longer he watched the two showgirls kiss, the more Pru filled his mind. The helpless way she'd succumbed to his touch. How it felt to be inside her, his length hugged tightly by her sweet core.

Not enough...

The two words whispered through his head as he watched the showgirls kiss. His manhood hanging limp between his legs, because no matter how hard they tried, the two of them weren't even half as sexy as Pru.

And now here he was, banging on Pru's door, not because he was drunk but because he was desperate to see her. It had been only two days, but he felt as if he was going out of his mind from missing her.

Unfortunately it wasn't Pru who answered the door, but her brother, in a pair of sweatpants, face screwed up with tired indignation.

"It's four in the morning. What the hell, man?" Jake demanded.

"Is Pru here?" Max asked. "I need to see her."

Jake shook his head and rubbed at his eyes, yawning as he answered, "You think I'd tell you? After what you did? Get out of here, man."

He started to close the door, but Max slammed one hand against it, halting its progress.

"How about if I said I loved her? Then would you go get her?"

Jake paused, not looking nearly as tired now. "I don't know. Is this some kind of messed-up hypothetical?"

Max shook his head. "No, I'm asking because it's true. This started off as a game. But no more games, Jake. Please go get her, and tell her she's ruined me for any other woman. Tell her I love her, and it's not about the money. It's about her. Me wanting to be with her, I've changed. She's changed me. Please, just go tell her that."

Jake studied him with a frown that made him look way older than his age. "You serious?" he asked.

"Dead serious," Max answered, his voice steady. Even though admitting that he loved a woman, one who might never love him back, terrified him.

But it was true. Every single word he'd said was true, and it must have shown on his face. After a few moments of shrewd observation, Jake actually reached down to what must have been a table just to the left of the door and produced a smartphone.

"Okay, I believe you," he said while typing something into the phone. "And I don't blame you. Pru's pretty great. Better than you deserve anyway."

"If you go get her, I will do everything in my power to convince both her and you to give me another chance," Max answered, once again knowing that what he said was 100 percent true.

But if Jake was impressed by his conviction, it didn't show. He just kept typing, his mouth set in a skeptical twist. "And how about all that stuff you were saying about me at BIT?" he asked without looking up. "Were you serious about my chances of making it out there?"

Max shrugged. "Yeah, I was serious. Still am. That's why I invested in your college education."

Jake finally looked up from his phone. "What do you mean?" he asked. "I thought the deal between you and Pru was off."

"It is," Max said. "But that doesn't mean I didn't think you could hack it at BIT."

Max reached into his pants pocket and pulled out the set of Thunderbird keys he'd received from James Market's assistant earlier in the evening. "Here, consider this a late graduation gift."

Jake caught them but shook his head in confusion. "But the guy said you weren't the buyer."

"I wasn't. Sorley Greer was, and…"

Max took a deep breath. Here came the real secret. The one Max had never told anyone ever. "I'm Sorley Greer."

Jake just shook his head in confusion. "Is that supposed to mean something to me?"

"No, I guess not," Max answered with a wry lift of his eyebrows. "Sorley Greer runs what's called a private investment pool out of Ireland. My grandmother's Irish, so I was able to get dual citizenship. His investment pool does pretty well for itself. Started off with a few million twelve years ago, now it's closing in on a billion, which means it's time for it to make the jump and become a hedge fund. But to do that, I need a big infusion of capital, which is what I was going to use my trust for."

Jake shook his head. "I thought you were partying all over the place. When did you find time to start a hedge fund or an investment pool or whatever you're talking about?"

Max threw Jake a sardonic half smile. "The two kind of go hand in hand. I kept Sorley's identity a secret, convinced a few of my Max Benton friends to invest with him sight unseen. Boom, there's my start-up money. But nobody knows I'm Sorley. They just think I'm Max, the guy at all the hottest clubs. And do you know what nearly every single CEO of nearly every single corporation has in common? Kids. Rich kids. A lot of them like me. Burning through their allowances with a whole lot of fun. You'd be surprised what information comes down through the party vine. Stuff you can use to make the best possible investments if you know what you're looking for."

Jake stared at him, openmouthed.

"Yeah, I guess I'm a little smarter than I look," Max finished. "And I liked this move of yours with selling the car. Shows you've got what it takes to leverage your resources and make bold moves. So trust me when I tell you, you're a smart kid."

Jake snorted and lowered the phone. "Well, I still think you're a douche and not worthy of my sister—I don't care how rich or not dumb you really are. But I guess since Pru and I are trying to treat each other like adults now, I figured I should at least let her know you're here, looking to talk to her."

Max's heart soared. But then Jake just stood there.

Forcing Max to ask, "So are you going to go get her or what?"

Jake shook his head. "Nah, man. Can't. She's not here. But I sent her a text, telling her you're here and you want to talk."

"Not here?" Max repeated. It was four in the morning. Where the hell else could she be?

As if reading his mind, Jake shrugged. "I dunno. She called some guy named Gus on the phone after we finished with the paperwork. Asked if she could meet him, then left. Told me she wouldn't be home until tomorrow."

Max's heart froze. He'd finally come to the conclusion that he was in love with Pru. But apparently she hadn't come to the same conclusion about him, because the first thing she'd done after getting her brother's future settled was run to Gus.

Chapter 26

"Girl, you need to go back to bed. It's only breakfast, and you look like death warmed over," Sunny informed Pru as she took the seat across from her at one of the Sinclair Lodge common room's long tables. Her plate was filled high with food from the retreat's last breakfast buffet.

Pru took Sunny's admonishment in stride. Mostly because, though she'd yet to look at herself in a mirror, she knew Sunny was probably right. She was still in the old tracksuit she'd thrown on for yesterday's Thunderbird fix-up, which had turned out to be a sale. She'd gotten maybe an hour tops of sleep in Gus's room last night. And after the week she'd had with Max, she was discovering that her days of running at full steam on limited sleep were on their way out.

But Pru shook her head. "No, I just need another cup of coffee, and I'll be good to go."

Sunny pursed her lips and asked, "Are you done eating?"

Pru glanced down at the half-full plate of uneaten food and didn't feel the desire to finish it. "Yeah, I guess so. Is there something you need me to do?"

"Yes, go to sleep," Sunny answered.

She came around the table and took Pru by the elbow, yanking her out of her seat.

"No, seriously, Sunny," Pru whispered, trying to get her elbow back without causing a scene. "We're so close to proving who the saboteur is. Just a couple more hours with Gus, and I'll have everything I need on the guy."

Sunny ignored Pru's protest and pulled her toward the

stairs. "Cole's in with Gus now anyway. Whatever it is you think you have to do can wait until you've had a nap. Gus will still be here then."

"But—"

Sunny's expression became uncharacteristically dark. "Don't fight me on this, Pru," she said with a glare. "I've taken care of you when you refuse to take care of yourself for years, and don't think I'm going to stop now, just because I'm pregnant. I'm not nearly as delicate as Cole wants people to think, and I can and will drag you kicking and screaming up to a bed if you fight me on this."

Sunny had been with her domineering husband too long, Pru decided. She sounded exactly like him now. But she gave in nonetheless. Not just because she believed Sunny really would follow through on her threat, but also because she was too tired to fight with her.

Maybe Sunny was right, Pru thought, as she trudged up the stairs alongside her best friend. She'd take a nap, clear her mind, then go back downstairs to Gus's room.

He'd probably need a few hours to process the report an old Benton Girl who'd gone on to become a forensic lab assistant for the Las Vegas Metropolitan Police Department had sent her via email this morning anyway. She was just glad that Cole had volunteered to do the dirty work of telling Gus what was in it as opposed to leaving the job to Pru.

The more she thought about it, sleeping through what was sure to be a whole lot of drama sounded better and better by the second. But when Sunny stopped outside the door to the room she'd shared with Max, Pru went stiff.

"No, I don't think so," she said, shaking her head. "I'll sleep on one of the couches in the common room downstairs."

She wheeled around, but Sunny caught her arm before she could leave, her eyes narrowing. "Cole got it wrong, didn't he? You and Max—you weren't just pretending… you really liked him, didn't you?"

Pru shook her head. "I don't want to talk about this."

"I knew it!" Sunny's face lit up with a triumphant look. "I kept wondering how I could have been so wrong about you two, but that explains it. I can't wait to tell Cole I was right."

"Wait, what?" Pru asked. "What do you mean?"

Sunny shrugged. "After that crazy wedding of yours hit YouTube, Cole called me up to ask if I thought you and Max were really together. And I told him I absolutely believed you two were. I totally vouched for you."

"What?" Pru said. "Why would you do that? Why would you think Max and I were such a sure thing?"

Sunny shook her head as if the answer was obvious. "Because Max plays the part of the ridiculous playboy who doesn't care about anything or anybody, but I've always suspected he's deeper than that. And because I knew you before your parents died, Pru. I remember how fun you used to be."

Pru shook her head. "If by 'fun' you mean stupid, reckless and irresponsible."

Sunny's eyes crinkled with sardonic amusement. "No, Pru, by 'fun' I mean *fun*—like the girl who was always talking me into wild adventures. Remember when we got that unexpected three-day break because they needed to do emergency repairs on the stage, and you found those cheap last-minute tickets to Mexico?"

Pru did remember that. They'd spent the entire three days club crawling. And in the check-in line on the way back to Vegas, Pru had convinced some wealthy businessmen to upgrade all their tickets to first class. That meant the tequila had kept flowing all the way on the return flight to Las Vegas. They barely made it back before the curtain went up for the show.

Pru groaned now, remembering, "We were wrecked that night. I'm still trying to figure out how we even got through the show."

"But what a memory!" Sunny insisted. "Listen, girl, maybe one day you'll have a baby of your own, then you'll really understand. All that stupid stuff we did when we were younger, it's not anything to regret. You led me into some great stories back in the day. Now that I'm a boring wife and soon-to-be mother, I'm really glad you convinced me to have so much fun when we were younger."

"You're not boring," Pru assured her. Then she asked, "Really, that's what you think of the way I used to be?" She'd certainly never thought of herself that way.

"Yes, really," Sunny answered. "And that's why I thought you were perfect for Max. You're levelheaded but you really know how to have a good time. Exactly the kind of woman Max needs, and could maybe appreciate. Plus, you're smart and strong. You'd never let someone like Max walk all over you just because he's a Benton heir. *That's* why I vouched for you."

A cloud fell over Sunny's face. "I just underestimated Max. I really did think a woman like you could not only net him, but also bring him down to earth. Help him heal from his messed-up childhood. But I guess in the end, Max didn't want to be fixed or even mend what had gone wrong between him and Cole. He just wanted his money, so that he could continue to live however he pleased."

As much as Pru wanted to agree with Sunny, she said, "I don't think it's so much that he didn't want to mend things with Cole. A lot of what happened was because he was too scared to think he and Cole could be the real deal, brothers like they used to be. I think he wanted to prove to Cole that he was his own man. In Max's own way, he truly thought tricking him into signing off on the trust fund was the only way to do that. But I think if they want to, they could get past this, especially now with the new information that's come to light…"

Pru wasn't trying to put a silver lining on the situation for Sunny's sake. She really did believe what she said, that Max was capable of turning over a new leaf where his brother was concerned. Max was someone who could be so much bigger if he just put his mind and heart to it.

In either case, "I'm not sleeping in this room," she told Sunny.

But Sunny seemed to completely understand. "Okay, why don't you sleep in my room," she offered, tugging on her arm again. "I'll come get you for lunch."

Pru gave in with a nod, letting Sunny escort her down the hallway to the other master bedroom suite. She was so tired now, she couldn't even put up a fake protest as Sunny opened the door for her.

"Um, Pru…" Sunny said in front of her. "Let me guess, the guy you were looking into as the mole was Harrison."

Pru's eyes widened. "Yeah, that's exactly who. Did Cole tell you?"

Her question was answered by the sound of a gun cocking.

And Pru stopped short when she saw Harrison standing by Cole's open laptop. He'd obviously been going through it before Pru and Sunny walked in on him.

"Close the door!" he said to them, his voice menacing and low. "Close the door now!"

Chapter 27

By the time Max came barging into the common room full of Benton Group executives eating breakfast, he was no longer in a mending-fences kind of mood. In fact, his fists were both clenched in anticipation of what he expected to find. Gus wanted the woman he loved? Then he'd better be prepared to fight for her, because Max had come back to Utah fully prepared for battle.

However, Gus was nowhere to be found in the designated breakfast area. "Where's Gus?" he snarled at one of the execs he vaguely remembered as being in charge of human resources.

"I—I'm not sure," he answered.

"Take a guess," Max said between clenched teeth.

"I think he's still in his room with…" The executive trailed off, his cheeks reddening, as if he'd belatedly put together a possible cause for the dangerous look on Max's face.

That was all Max needed to hear. He headed toward the rooms at the back of the lodge and burst into Gus's without knocking.

Only to find him sitting on top of his bed with Cole seated across from him in a small desk chair.

They both looked up when he came into the room, surprise written across Gus's face and guilt on Cole's, which was shocking. Max had seen Cole look guilty only once before, when his relationship with Sunny had imploded in a bomb of secrets revealed.

"Okay, what's going on?" Max asked, carefully closing the door behind himself.

Gus didn't answer, just stared at Max. His eyes searched Max's face as if he were seeing him for the first time.

Weird, Max thought. He noticed Gus wasn't the clean-cut Southern gentleman version of himself that Max had become used to. Today, his hair looked as if it had been styled with a lawn mower, and there were dark circles under his eyes, as if he'd been up all night. With Pru? Max wondered, his gut going cold.

"Where's Pru? Jake said she was here." Max stared at Gus hard and added, "With you."

"She is here," Cole answered in Gus's stead. He stood up to face Max.

Cole paused, studying Max closely with a quizzical expression. Max guessed it was because they hadn't exactly parted on great terms.

"It's also true that she came here to see Gus," Cole further explained.

Cole stopped, watching Max closely.

Max's eyes stayed on Gus. "So she was with you last night?"

Before Gus could answer, Cole once again interrupted. "The real question is, why do you care that she was with Gus last night? It's not like you have to pretend to be in love with her anymore."

Max's jaw set. "I wasn't pretending," he admitted quietly. "Not about that."

Cole's eyes narrowed. "Is this another trick, Max?" he asked. "Because if it is…"

Max cut him off. "Don't bother threatening me, Cole. I'm not here for you. I'm here for Pru and Pru only. Because I love her, and unfortunately I didn't realize that until it was too late. But believe me, I get it now, and I'm here."

He then turned back toward Gus. "And I plan to take out anyone who tries to get between us."

Gus stood up, shaking his head. "Look, normally I'd be down to scrap with you over this. But not this morning, man. Not after the night I had with Pru."

Max started to advance to Gus, but Cole got in front of him, his hands raised in the air. "Understand that Gus is extremely tired right now. In this case he's being serious, not trying to bait you. Pru's made two breaks on the case. First she figured out it wasn't Gus sabotaging the business, but Harrison, and she needed Gus to help her get the proof she needed. He has access to all of Harrison's work accounts, thanks to the training they'd done all summer. That's why he and Pru were up all night. They were here together, but as far as I know, nothing happened."

Max looked to Gus. "That true?"

Gus shrugged. "Yeah, it's true. Nothing happened, unless you call me watching her on my computer all night, something."

Max's shoulders sagged with relief. "And what was the other thing?"

Cole looked from Gus to Max. Then from Max to Gus. "She also figured out why Granddad took such an early interest in Gus. She followed a hunch and got a few strands of Gus's hair from a hairbrush and a few strands of yours and had them analyzed by a friend of hers who works in forensics. Apparently, Gus is your brother."

Max blinked. Then blinked some more. Then said, "What do you mean, my brother? You're my brother. My only brother."

"Not *our* brother," Cole said, as if reading his mind. "Pru thought so at first, and she came up here to break the news to Gus and get some of my DNA for analysis, too. But the more she looked into it, the more she became convinced he was only your half brother. Gus was born less than five months after your mother left you with Gran and Granddad."

Every thing became clear to Max then. Why his mother

had so abruptly dropped him off with her in-laws. Why she hadn't come back for so much as a visit until nearly a year later.

She'd seemed different the next time Max had seen her. Unsteady. As if the prescription drugs she consumed by the handful, tossed back with wine, were the only things keeping her together. This would become her MO over the next few years. Coming to Las Vegas for visits, all smiles and bearing gifts, only to become more and more frantic over the course of her stay. Until one day, he'd wake up and there'd be a note slipped under his door, about how she'd decided to go meet friends or a lover in a place that wasn't Las Vegas. In a place that wasn't anywhere near Max.

Max stared at Gus now. Apparently he hadn't even gotten that. Their mother had abandoned him from day one with a heart condition and a father who would eventually die, leaving him with no one.

Gus took the story from there. "Pru put all the clues together. I don't like to talk about it, but I had a pretty hard upbringing, with occasional windfalls of luck. An anonymous donor paid for my heart surgery when I was a kid. And I got the Benton Foundation scholarship, even though my grades weren't all that great…and I didn't apply for it. Back then, I figured it was because my guidance counselor liked me—she was always telling me I could be so much more if I just applied myself."

Max lifted an eyebrow. He'd had similar conversations with his own guidance counselor. Apparently they'd had a few things in common as teenagers despite growing up worlds apart.

"When I got that scholarship, I figured she must have been the one who put me up for it—maybe even fudged my grades so I'd get it. And I didn't want to get her in trouble, so I went on ahead and applied to Cornell. I was as surprised as anybody else when I actually got in. But back then I thought it must have been because I already had the scholarship. Same goes for when your grandpa recruited me for the Benton New Orleans. I thought it all went together."

Cole stepped in then to explain, "And that's why he didn't brag about the scholarship or being recruited by Granddad. He didn't necessarily deserve the scholarship in the first place."

"That's also why I worked so hard when I got to the Benton New Orleans," Gus told them. "Trust me, I know where I was headed before that scholarship came along, and it paved a new road for me."

Max nodded, believing Gus's story and putting together his own conclusions about his grandfather's actions. Yeah, that would have been Granddad's response to finding out Max had a half brother in New Orleans. He was too stodgy to take in a kid who wasn't related to him by blood, but too sentimental not to help the kid out when he could.

"So…" Max said, sizing up Gus in a new light. "You're my brother."

Gus also seemed to be sizing him up. "Yeah, I guess I am."

Max suddenly found himself smiling. Smiling bigger than he would have guessed over the prospect of having another half brother. All this time, he'd been resentful of being Cole's little brother. Now he was going to get to be someone's big brother.

"All right," Max said, slapping his hands together. "First things first. We find Pru and tell her that we both obviously have good taste. But I'm the brother she's going to need to choose because I'm in love with her."

Gus nodded, a tired but game smile lifting his lips up. "All right. I guess I can play a part in this rom-com you've got going on with her."

Max grinned back at him. "Awesome, glad that's settled." He then strung an arm around his little brother's shoulders and led him toward the door. "Second thing we need to talk about is you coming to work for me in New

Orleans at the hotel I'm putting together. This trip has made me realize that I'll probably be needing a partner to run the hotel's day-to-day business, and I think you're just the guy."

"Wait, what?" said Cole behind them.

"Seriously?" Gus asked at the same time.

"Yeah, seriously, man," Max answered, opening the door and leading Gus out of the room. "I mean, you took a hit on that first presentation, but then you came back and killed it. I need someone like you. Someone who knows how to take punches and get on board with new ideas."

"Max, what hotel?" Cole demanded behind them.

"Come up to my room, so we can talk terms," Max said, leading Gus toward the stairs. "I'm not stingy like Cole. I'll do more than give you a few shares. I'll make you a partner, even let you choose your own title."

"Are you serious?" Gus asked, his eyes widening.

"Are you serious?" Cole asked at the same time behind him.

"Yep," Max said as he walked up the stairs beside Gus. He was definitely going to like this big-brother business.

Cole followed them, his voice hard and demanding as he said, "Tell me you are not starting a rival hotel in New Orleans."

"This hotel won't be remotely in the same league as a stodgy old Benton hotel," Max answered Cole over his shoulder.

"That's what you were planning to do with your trust money? Start a hotel?" Gus asked.

"One of the things," Max answered, deciding to save his hedge-fund expansion for later. "Thing is, you've got a couple of decades under Cole at the Benton Group before you even get close to the number of shares you'd need to make your voice count. But if you quit the Benton Las Vegas and come operate this hotel with me in New Orleans, then you get to be your own man. So two decades slogging under Cole, or taking charge of your life by going in with me on this start-up? One is sure to be boring and one is sure to be an adventure, but you know, your choice, man."

"He chooses the Benton Group, one of the fastest-growing and most respected brands in the hotel industry," Cole answered for Gus.

Gus looked intrigued.

His lack of a quick refusal set Cole off in a way Max hadn't experienced in a while. His older brother grabbed him by the arm and said, "If you think I'm going to let you use your trust fund to build a competing hotel and steal my new vice president, you must not know me, Max."

The sinister note in Cole's voice touched Max to his very core, and he actually had to work hard to keep a goofy smile off his face.

Cole didn't go all menacing businessman on just anybody. With Max and nearly anyone else of whom he didn't approve, he was usually just coldly contemptuous. No, this arch-villain voice of his was on exclusive reserve for his business rivals—which meant he now considered Max a true rival.

But two could play the arch-villain game. Max took his arm back, opening his mouth to inform Cole that he had enough financial and social capital to get the hotel funded with or without his trust fund. But then he was interrupted by the sound of a gunshot ringing out, cold and deadly, through the lodge.

Chapter 28

"Sunny, run!" Pru screamed at her best friend as she struggled with Harrison.

She'd taken a calculated risk that Harrison was holding them at gunpoint only to give himself enough time to escape the scene. Pru didn't think he truly wanted to harm either of them—especially the pregnant Sunny.

She'd then gotten as close as possible under the guise of trying to reason with Harrison. Like most secretly malcontented employees, he had a lot to say about why he'd decided to double-cross the company that had been signing his checks for nearly three decades.

The whole story had come out, angrily and desperately. He had gone on about how "that cheap bastard" Cole had awarded him only a few shares in the Benton Group when it had gone public.

But the last straw had been when Cole had hired a thirty-year-old boy to replace him. That, Harrison just couldn't abide. So he'd struck a deal with the Benton Inn's biggest potential rival. And then that deal had gone to hell when his contact at Key Card accused him of giving them bad information on purpose and opening Key Card up to a possible defamation suit if the blogger he'd tipped off squealed. His Key Card contact had threatened to expose Harrison to Cole and the authorities if he didn't get him something else—something Key Card could really use. According to Harrison, he'd been left with no choice but to break into Cole's room while he and Sunny were both otherwise occupied.

"Who wouldn't have done what I did in my position?" he'd whined to Pru.

Pru could think of a lot of people who wouldn't have turned on their employer of thirty years. But she'd met people like Harrison before. People who went on and on about how nice they were and made big splashy shows of giving money to charity. Not because they actually gave a damn about the cause, but because they wanted everyone else to know what nice guys they were. However, in Pru's experiences, supposed "nice guys" often felt even more entitled than "bad boys" like Max.

How many times had Pru been aggressively hit on by tourists, claiming she should come back to their hotel room because they were such nice guys?

But Pru listened to Harrison's self-indulgent sob story. Listened and drew closer as she did.

Then she kneed the "nice guy," who currently had a gun trained on her pregnant friend, in the balls at the same time that she pushed his gun arm into the air.

He fell forward with an indignant yell. Luckily the gun was in the air, because he squeezed the trigger, sending plaster from the ceiling spraying down on them.

"Sunny, run!" Pru yelled as she struggled with Harrison to get control of the gun.

"No! No!" he screamed. "Let me go. You bitch!"

He was the same height as Pru, but still a man. It was taking all her strength to keep his wrist in the air. Plus, Harrison had the adrenaline of panic and unexpected pain on his side.

"Sunny, run!" she yelled again, hoping that her friend had managed to clear the room, because she didn't know how much longer she could hold on.

A huge body suddenly came out of nowhere, blocking her view of Harrison.

Now Harrison really screamed.

Pru stumbled back and watched Max take the gun off

Harrison as if it was a piece of candy he was prying from a baby's hand. The next thing Pru knew, Harrison was lying facedown on the floor with Max's knee in his back and his own revolver pressed against his temple.

Max looked up at Pru then. "You okay?" His voice was deadly calm, but there was murder in his pale green eyes. As if Harrison's continued existence depended on her answer.

"I'm fine," Pru assured him quickly.

Pru suddenly remembered Sunny and looked around wildly, only to find her outside the doorway crying in Cole's arms. A rush of relief flooded over her. She then brought her eyes back to Max.

For a moment their eyes stayed locked, her fear giving away to gratitude. She was safe now. They all were. Because of Max.

Chapter 29

Many hours later, Pru, Max, Sunny, Gus and Cole found themselves alone in the Sinclair Lodge's downstairs sitting room. Cole, Max and Pru had matching tumblers of whiskey. They'd all been filled by Sunny, who, though unable to partake, had insisted that they needed something after hours of answering local law enforcement's questions about what had happened in the master bedroom, which had now been taped off as an official crime scene.

Pru carefully sipped on her whiskey, thinking about how many things had been resolved over the course of the day. Gus and Max now knew they were brothers, and Cole had officially declared the executive retreat over. Harrison and the police had vacated the lodge—along with the rest of the Benton execs, most of whom were happy to leave early after discovering there had been a dangerous traitor in their midst the entire week.

But the main point was that everyone was safe now, and perhaps that was why Pru felt so at peace.

Max, however, had been uncharacteristically quiet since the police had arrived and taken over with Harrison. Pensive, as if he was still wondering if he should have pulled the trigger. Pru was glad he hadn't, but could understand the inclination. Harrison had turned into a wild card in those last few moments of their standoff and she was just happy everyone got out unharmed.

Still, she watched Max, who was standing by the window now, his whiskey remaining untouched. She was worried about him.

"Pru."

Cole's voice dragged Pru's gaze away from Max.

Cole had an arm around his pregnant wife, who was nursing a cup of tea. "I want you to know that I'm very grateful," he told her. "Not only because you solved the case, but also because of the selfless way you put Sunny's life before your own."

"You shouldn't have put yourself in danger like that," Sunny chimed in, "but thank you, thank you from the bottom of my heart."

Pru shook her head, refusing to accept their gratitude. "Thank Max. He's the one who wrestled Harrison to the ground."

Max came away from the window then, shaking his head in adamant denial. "If that gun hadn't gone off, we might never have known you needed our help," he pointed out. "You could have been taken out of here by that maniac, without us even knowing."

Pru started to protest again, but Max growled. "Take the credit, Pru. You deserve it."

"Yes, you do," Cole said, for once agreeing with his brother. "Which is why I want to offer you something I rarely promise. A favor. Anything you need, no matter how big or small, I'm prepared to grant it."

Pru set down her glass on the coffee table in front of the couch. "Really? Anything?"

Cole nodded gravely. "Yes, anything. Just name it."

Pru didn't have to think long. "I want you to give Max his trust money without any strings attached."

Cole blinked. "What?" he said, his arm dropping from around Sunny's shoulders.

"It's his money, and even though I'm still not cool with the word *deserve* after what happened with Harrison, the fact is your grandfather left it to him. It's his birthright, and you shouldn't mess with that."

Pru could feel Max's eyes on her, but she kept her own

eyes on Cole, who was now sitting straight up on the couch, his face tight with irritation. "So let me get this straight. The favor you're requesting is that I sign off on Max's trust, so that he can build a rival hotel to the Benton New Orleans?"

Pru looked at Max, her eyes widening. "You told him?"

Max looked back at her, his own expression unreadable. "Yeah, I told him."

Pru threw him a little smile. She was glad Max was communicating more with his brother, but she refused to back down from her initial request. This was the right thing to do, and the only action that would end the battle of wills between the two Benton brothers.

She turned back to Cole. "You said anything."

Cole opened his mouth. Then snapped it closed. Something ticked in his jaw for a few seconds, and then finally he let out a sound of disgust. "Fine, if you want to waste your one favor on Max. That's fine, I suppose."

He glared at Max but started toward the lodge's front door. "C'mon out to the car with me. I packed the paperwork in my luggage when the police told us to get everything we needed out of the room before they taped it off. You can look through it while my assistant arranges for a notary to come up here—"

"No." Max didn't follow Cole. Just said the one word while continuing to stare at Pru.

"What do you mean no?" Pru and Cole asked him at the same time.

"No," Max said again, barely able to believe the words were coming out of his mouth. "I don't want the money."

Pru stood up now, looking at him as if he'd gone crazy. "What do you mean you don't want the money? That was the whole reason you married me, and that's the deal for our prenup—we only have to stay married until you get your trust money."

"Exactly," Max answered. "That's why I don't want the money. Not if it means you get to divorce me."

Pru shook her head. "I don't understand—"

"I love you, Pru," he said. "Do you understand that? *I love you.* You challenge me. You're sexy as hell, and I've had more fun with you at this boring executive retreat in Utah than I've had with any other girl ever. I meant every word I said to you the night before Jake came up here, and I want us to stay together. I want you to move to New Orleans with me after Jake goes away to BIT. Because I love you. I love you so much, I don't care about using my trust to build my hotel, because I'm not going to build it if you're not going to share the penthouse suite with me when it's done."

Pru stared at him, her eyes wide with shock. Max opened his mouth, fully prepared to pour more words over the situation, as many as it took to make her believe he was dead serious about this.

But Pru cut him off with a shake of her head. "No, Max," she insisted. "I want you to sign those papers."

He took a step toward her, but she moved away before he could so much as touch her.

"I'm serious. I'm not saying another word to you until you sign those papers. Then I can go back to Las Vegas and file for a divorce, ending this sham of a marriage."

He started to take another step toward her. But he knew anything he said would be useless. Yes, he loved her, but that didn't mean she loved him back or ever would after what he'd done.

Max's jaw set. He did love her, which meant that he'd do anything. Anything it took to make her happy. If she didn't want to be with him…he realized in those moments he had to let her go.

He looked over at Cole. "How fast can we get a notary here?"

Pretty fast as it turned out. Less than forty minutes later, all the necessary paperwork was signed. Max had a spoken guarantee from Cole that the sum of his trust would be delivered into his bank account within the next few days.

After the business was all done, Max turned to Pru, who for some reason still hadn't left. Maybe because she wanted to make sure she'd be free to divorce him without penalty, he thought.

"There, it's done," he said. Then, because he, too, was learning to keep his promises, he added through clenched teeth, "I'll have my lawyer draw up the divorce papers. It'll take a few weeks. Six tops. But I'll sign and have him send them to you immediately after."

The smile Pru gave him was positively beatific, as if he'd just granted her most fervent wish. "Good. But I won't be living in Las Vegas six weeks from now. I'll give you my new address. Tell him to send it to me, care of my boyfriend, Sorley Greer, at—I'm not sure what that hotel's address is in New Orleans. Do you have it on you?"

Max smiled. "You knew?"

She came to stand in front of him. "Almost from the beginning," she informed him. "In New Orleans, you said Sorley Greer was your college roommate, but I knew you didn't have a college roommate. I did some digging after agreeing to marry you."

Max had no idea why he'd believed Pru might not solve Cole's case even for a minute. As it turned out, she was extremely thorough at her job. No wonder she'd been so emphatic about him being a liar. She'd known this whole time, known and probably wondered why getting the trust had been so important to him. Then she'd figured out why before he'd even had it all figured out himself. Figured it out and then explained it all to him so that he understood, too.

He knew then that he wasn't being crazy when it came to Pru. Nobody else got him as this girl did, and nobody else ever would.

"Detective Pru caught me," he said. "And that's why

you're refusing to stay married to me, because you think I'm a liar."

Her face softened. "No, I'm refusing to stay married to you because Detective Pru is practical. Too practical to let you give up your inheritance just to prove you love me, and too practical to stay married to a guy I've only really known for, like, a week."

She broke off with another grin. "*But* there's still enough of the Old Pru left in me to take a gamble on moving in with you in New Orleans. And Sorley Greer is much more Detective Pru's speed, so there's a good chance this might all work out after all."

She laid her hands on his chest and peeked up at him. "Luckily we both have two people inside us. I guess it was meant to be."

Max more than guessed. As he drew Pru into his arms and gave her the kiss that would officially begin a new phase of their relationship, he knew. Knew that Pru and he were a sure bet.

Somewhere in the distance he heard Sunny say, "Oh, my gosh, this is so romantic."

Right before Cole said, "Wait a minute. *You're* Sorley Greer?"

Epilogue

"No, Max, I don't want to marry you! I really, really don't!" Pru yelled.

Her refusal might have been taken a little bit more seriously if she wasn't buck naked, clinging to the edge of the new bed she'd picked out with Max for the penthouse suite just a few weeks ago. And if Max didn't already have a firm grip around both her ankles, in the midst of literally dragging her out of that bed.

"Too late. Today's the day. And we've got two hundred people, including press, due in just a few hours to witness the big event." The brass bed frame groaned as Max tugged on her legs again.

"Let's just call it off," Pru insisted, clawing the mattress. "That will get us more press than doing another nightclub wedding."

"First of all, my business partner would kill me. He's invited just about every press outlet in New Orleans to this shindig."

"Gus will understand," Pru said. "He's much more reasonable than you when it comes to publicity stunts like this. That's why you two make such a good team."

Pru was wheedling to get her way, but it was true. Between Max's social savvy and Gus's dedication to grind work, they'd gotten The Sorley up and running in record time. It was a feat that truly deserved celebration in Pru's proud opinion—just not with another crazy wedding extravaganza to kick off The Sorley's soft open.

"Besides, we're already married," she pointed out.

Somehow in the year since they'd moved to New Orleans together, despite her near-constant reminders toward the beginning of her stay, Max had never gotten around to asking his lawyers to put together their divorce papers. And now it was too late.

The hotel was ready to open, and instead of a divorce, Max had somehow talked her into a second stunt wedding, this one even crazier than the first.

Looking over her shoulder at the man who was still her husband, she sometimes didn't know where the surprisingly consummate businessman ended and her ridiculously obstinate lover began.

"Getting married again purely for the press doesn't make any sense," she said, trying to get through to the reasonable man who also ran a successful hedge fund and had somehow convinced Cole Benton to allow The Sorley to go up without a dirty business fight. Not only that, but he'd also gotten his older brother to silently invest money from the Benton Group into The Sorley by pointing out that it would be the beginning of a possible cycle, attracting young people who'd eventually have families and move on to the Benton Inn. Then eventually on to the Benton New Orleans, when they grew older and once again had more income at their disposal.

"It's a waste of money, don't you think?" she asked, trying to appeal to Sorley, Max's more logical side.

Her ankles were abruptly released and Pru's body hit the mattress with a little bounce. But her release was short-lived. As soon as she let go of the mattress, thinking Max had finally seen reason, he picked her up off the bed and twisted her around until her body was fully cradled in his strong arms.

"Max…" she started, struggling to get back out of his arms.

"I see what's happening here," he said, walking over to

the bright red couch, which was shaped like a pair of lips. "You're holding out for further convincing."

Pru's cheeks heated. True, he'd gotten her to agree to another outrageous wedding after a particularly body-rocking night of lovemaking. "Max, this isn't about—"

"You know, I once had a dream about you naked on this couch. Let's make that dream come true."

He let her go, and Pru yelped as she landed on the red couch in a naked heap. Max soon followed, using his hands and mouth on her in such a way that she definitely knew whom she was dealing with now—the man who had ruined her for any other.

He took his time, once again laying down his argument with kisses, caressing her most sensitive spots until she was quivering with need. And begging him to stop teasing her with desperate whispers.

He gave her what she wanted, sitting on the couch and pulling her on top of him. But when he was inside her, instead of letting her ride, as she thought he might, he hugged her closer, anchoring her body on his so that he could guide the action.

Pru was happy to let him do it. She bit down on her lip as he rocked into her, filling her up to her very core, with his base pressed into the hot button at her center.

She didn't last long in this position, and she screamed out his name before bursting into a million stars. Vaguely she registered him coming soon after. Max, her companion in all things, she thought with a happy smile.

After he was done, he stroked one hand into her hair, curving it around the back of her neck. Her hair was a little longer now, getting big in its natural state, and she could feel some of the curls his hand displaced on the lower part of her neck.

"Pru, I love you," he said, the look on his face both somber and tender.

Making it so Pru doubted she could have denied how she felt, even if she'd wanted to. "I love you, too," she answered.

"Will you marry me?" he asked her. "Again? Tonight? Just like I planned?"

"Yes," she answered, thoroughly enchanted by the look in his pale green eyes.

"Good," he said, patting her naked backside before lifting her off him and setting her aside on the couch. "Because Sunny's waiting for you downstairs."

"What? Sunny? What's she doing here?" she demanded, her voice rising a few pitches.

"Dunno." Max stood up and headed for the closet. "Something about missing the first wedding, and how could we even think about excluding her, Cole and Nora from the second one. Especially since I named Gus my best man over Cole."

"Wait, Gus is the best man now?" she asked.

"Yeah, we had to balance it out, since Sunny's your matron of honor," Max answered as if it was obvious. "I was hoping to make little Berta the flower girl, but no dice. Cole says the kid's still not walking."

He disappeared into the large closet to the left of their bathroom.

"Maybe because she's only nine months!" Pru called after him, quickly coming to their goddaughter's defense. "And I can't believe you would invite a child to a nightclub wedding—or your grandmother!"

"Whatever. Gran's just happy she gets to see the wedding outfit this time," he answered from inside the closet. "She even offered to loan you another one of her old costumes. But I told her we already had your wedding outfit shipped from Vegas."

Pru rubbed her eyes, tired at just the thought of the scanty showgirl costumes she'd have to wear for this event.

"Seriously, I don't know if I can act like a wild party girl in front of your family. I think we should call this off."

Max poked his head out of the closet to answer, "But Jake flew all the way out here for this."

And Pru did a double-take. "You invited Jake. You invited *my brother*!"

She waved her hands in front of her face just thinking about it. True, she had learned over the past year to start treating Jake like an adult, especially after he had chosen a summer job at the Benton Las Vegas over coming to stay with her and Max in New Orleans. But this was a line she totally refused to cross. She'd never even let her brother see a Benton Revue show, and she sure as heck wasn't going to act a fool for the press in front of him.

"I won't do it," she told Max, covering her eyes. "I won't fake marry you, wearing a showgirl costume, in front of my brother."

"Okay, how about wearing this?" Max asked.

She uncovered her eyes to see Max now standing outside the closet door, holding up a hanger with a maxi dress hanging on it. The dress was made of ivory lace, off the shoulder, with a lovely ruffled overlay. It was definitely a vintage dress, one Pru recognized immediately, even though she hadn't seen it in years. Not since she and her brother had moved from a house to an apartment and put most of their parents' things into storage.

It was her mother's wedding dress.

Pru covered her mouth with one hand, tears slipping down her cheeks. "It's not a fake wedding, is it?"

Max shook his head, the usual wicked gleam in his eyes gone. "No, I want you to marry me, Prudence Washington. For real this time. Will you spend the rest of your life with me? Say yes, sweetheart."

"Yes," she whispered, with no hesitation.

She'd gambled her heart when she'd agreed to come with Max to New Orleans. But looking at the man she'd soon be marrying in front of her dearest friends and family, she knew for certain that love gamble had paid off.

And even more so, that once she'd gone Max, she'd never, ever go back.

* * * * *

REQUEST YOUR FREE BOOKS!

2 FREE NOVELS
PLUS 2 FREE GIFTS!

KIMANI™
ROMANCE

Love's ultimate destination!

YES! Please send me 2 FREE Harlequin® Kimani™ Romance novels and my 2 FREE gifts (gifts are worth about $10). After receiving them, if I don't wish to receive any more books, I can return the shipping statement marked "cancel." If I don't cancel, I will receive 4 brand-new novels every month and be billed just $5.44 per book in the U.S. or $5.99 per book in Canada. That's a savings of at least 16% off the cover price. It's quite a bargain! Shipping and handling is just 50¢ per book in the U.S. and 75¢ per book in Canada.* I understand that accepting the 2 free books and gifts places me under no obligation to buy anything. I can always return a shipment and cancel at any time. Even if I never buy another book, the two free books and gifts are mine to keep forever.

168/368 XDN GH4P

Name	(PLEASE PRINT)

Address	Apt. #

City	State/Prov.	Zip/Postal Code

Signature (if under 18, a parent or guardian must sign)

Mail to the **Reader Service:**

IN U.S.A.: P.O. Box 1867, Buffalo, NY 14240-1867
IN CANADA: P.O. Box 609, Fort Erie, Ontario L2A 5X3

Want to try two free books from another line?
Call 1-800-873-8635 or visit www.ReaderService.com.

* Terms and prices subject to change without notice. Prices do not include applicable taxes. Sales tax applicable in N.Y. Canadian residents will be charged applicable taxes. Offer not valid in Quebec. This offer is limited to one order per household. Not valid for current subscribers to Harlequin® Kimani™ Romance books. All orders subject to credit approval. Credit or debit balances in a customer's account(s) may be offset by any other outstanding balance owed by or to the customer. Please allow 4 to 6 weeks for delivery. Offer available while quantities last.

Your Privacy—The Reader Service is committed to protecting your privacy. Our Privacy Policy is available online at www.ReaderService.com or upon request from the Reader Service.

We make a portion of our mailing list available to reputable third parties that offer products we believe may interest you. If you prefer that we not exchange your name with third parties, or if you wish to clarify or modify your communication preferences, please visit us at www.ReaderService.com/consumerschoice or write to us at Reader Service Preference Service, P.O. Box 9062, Buffalo, NY 14240-9062. Include your complete name and address.